Brides and Sinners in El Chuco

Camino del Sol

A Latina and Latino Literary Series

Brides and and Sinners in El Chuco

Short Stories

by

Christine Granados

The University of Arizona Press
Tucson

The University of Arizona Press
© 2006 Christine Granados
All rights reserved

∞ This book is printed on acid–free, archival–quality paper.
Manufactured in the United States of America

11 10 09 08 07 06   6 5 4 3 2 1

Library of Congress Cataloging–in–Publication Data
Granados, Christine, 1969–
Brides and sinners in El Chuco : short stories / by
Christine Granados.
p. cm. – (Camino del sol)
ISBN–13: 978-0-8165-2492-1 (pbk. : acid–free paper)
ISBN–10: 0-8165-2492-0 (pbk. : acid–free paper)
1. El Paso (Tex.)–Fiction. 2. Problem families–Fiction.
3. Domestic fiction, American. 4. Young women–Fiction.
I. Title. II. Series.
PS3607.R3624B75 2006
813'.6–dc22
2005017333

Publication of this book is made possible in part by
the proceeds of a permanent endowment created with the
assistance of a Challenge Grant from the National Endowment
for the Humanities, a federal agency.

To Esten and our boys,

who taught me how to love.

Contents

Brides and Sinners in El Chuco

The Bride

When the month of June rolls around, I have to buy the five-pound bride magazine off the rack at the grocery store. The photographs of white dresses, articles with to-do lists, and advertisements for wedding planners remind me of my older sister Rochelle's wedding. She had been planning for her special day as far back as I can remember. Every year when she was a child, Rochelle dressed as a beautiful, blushing bride for Halloween. She sauntered her way down the hot, dusty streets of El Paso, accepting candy from our neighbors in her drawstring handbag. The white satin against Rochelle's olive skin made her look so pretty that I didn't mind the fact that we had to stop every three houses so she could empty the candy from her dainty bag into the ripped brown paper sack that I used for the journey. She had to drag me along with her—a reluctant Caspar—because Mom made her, and because I could hold all her candy. Her thick black hair was braided, and she wore the trenzas in an Eva Perón-style moño. She spent hours in the bathroom, with her friend Prissy fixing her hair just right, only to cover her head with a white tulle veil.

As Rochelle did this, Mom would prepare my costume. Spent and uninspired after a long day at work, Mom would drape a sheet over me and cut out holes for eyes. It happened every year without fail. The fact that I couldn't make up my mind what I wanted to be for Halloween exasperated my already exhausted mother even more. In a matter of minutes, I would list the Bionic Woman, a wrestler, a linebacker, a fat man, all as potential getups before it was time to trick-or-treat.

Ro, on the other hand, had her bridal dress finished days in advance, and she'd wear it to school to show it off. When people opened their doors to us, they would say, "Ay, qué bonita la novia, and your little brother un fantasma tan scary." I'd have to clear things up at every house with "I'm not a boy." They would laugh and ask Rochelle if she had a husband. She would giggle and give them a name.

When she got too old for Halloween, she started getting serious about planning her own wedding. She bought bride magazines and drew up plans, leaving absolutely no detail unattended. When it finally did happen, it was nothing like she had expected.

Rochelle was obsessed. Because all those ridiculous magazines never listed mariachis or dollar dances, she decided her wedding was going to have a string quartet, no bajo, horns, or anything, no dollar dance, and it was going to be in October. It was going to be a bland affair, outside in a tent, like the weddings up North in the "elegance of autumn" that she read about in the thick glossy pages of the magazines. I wasn't going to tell her there is no "elegance" to autumn in El Paso. Autumn is either "scramble a huevo on the hood of your car hot," or wind so strong the sand it blows stings your face and arms.

In the magazine pictures, all the people were white, skinny, and rich. All the women wore linen or silk slips that draped over their skeletal frames, and the men wore tuxedos or black suits and ties. She didn't take into account that in those pages, there was no tía Trini, who we called Teeny because, at five-foot-two, she weighed at least three hundred pounds. The slip dress Rochelle wanted everyone to wear would be swallowed in Teeny's cavernous flesh. And I never saw anyone resembling tío Lacho, who wore the burgundy tuxedo he got married in, two sizes too small, to every family wedding. The guests in the magazine weddings were polite and refined, with their long-stemmed wineglasses half full. No one ever got falling-down drunk and picked a fight, like Pilar. He would get so worked up someone would have to knock him out with a bottle of El Presidente. He was proud of the scars on his head, too, showing them off just before the big fight started.

Rochelle wanted tall white boys with jawbones that looked like they had been chiseled from stone to be her groomsmen; never mind the fact that we knew only one white boy, and he had acne so bad his face was blue. She also wanted her maid of honor to be pencil thin, although she would never admit it. Still, she was always dropping hints, telling her best friend, Prissy, that by the time they were twenty all their baby fat would be gone, and they would both look fabulous in their silk gowns. Never mind the fact that I, two years younger than Rochelle, could encircle my sister's bicep between my middle finger and thumb, and that Prissy rested her Tab colas on her huge stomach when she sat. My sister was in denial. And it wasn't just about her obese friend but about her entire life. She thought that if she planned every last detail of her wedding on paper, she could change who she was, who we were. Her lists drove me crazy.

She kept a running tally of the songs to be played by the band, adding and deleting as her musical tastes changed through the years. She carefully selected the food to be served to her guests. She resolutely decided what everyone in the family would be wearing. She even painstakingly chose what her dress would look like, down to the last sequin. But in order to marry, she needed a groom. And she was just as diligent about finding one as she was about the rest of the affair.

Every night before going to bed, she would pull out her pink wedding notebook and scratch a boy's name off her list of potential husbands. She went through two notebooks in one year. She was always on the lookout for husbands. One time, Rochelle and I spent an entire Saturday morning typing up fake raffle tickets to sell to Mike, who lived two blocks over. Ro had never met Mike, but she liked his broad shoulders—thought they'd look good in a tuxedo. So she made up a story that she was helping me sell raffle tickets for my softball team. Ro didn't let little things, like the truth, get in the way of her future. All the money raised would go into the team's travel budget. She even made up first-, second-, and third-place prizes. First place would be a color TV, second place, a dinner for two at Fortis Mexican Food Restaurant, and third, two tickets to the movies. She said Mike was going to win third place, and when she delivered his prize, she was going to suggest he take her to the movies since she was the one who sold him the winning ticket. I thought my sister was a genius, until we got to the door and knocked. When Mike answered, Ro delivered her lines like she had been selling raffle tickets all day long. When he told us he had no money, we were shocked. Ro didn't have a Plan B. Then, when his older brother came to the door and offered to buy all ten of the raffle tickets, we were speechless. All we could do was take his money, give him his stubs, and wish him luck. Ro was so upset her plan was a failure that she let me keep the ten dollars. Needless to say, Mike got scratched off her list.

Her blue notebook was where she compiled her guest list and either added or deleted a name depending on what had happened in school that day. I got scratched out six times in one month: for using all her sanitary napkins as elbow and knee pads while skating; for wearing her real silver concho belt and losing it at school; for telling Mom that Rochelle was giving herself hickeys on her arms; for peeking in her diary; for feeding her goldfish, Hughie, so much that he died; and especially, for telling her the truth about the food she planned to serve at her wedding. That final act kept me off the list for two months straight. She wanted finger foods like in Anglo weddings—sandwiches with the crusts cut off.

"Those cream cheese and cucumber sandwiches aren't going to cut it, Ro," I said through the cotton shirt I was taking off.

"My wedding is going to be classy," she yelled at me from across the room, where she was sitting on top of her bed, smoothing lotion on her arms. "If you don't want to eat my food, then you just won't be invited."

I laughed. Her nostrils were flaring pretty steady, and she was winding her middle finger around her ponytail. Then she reached under the mattress for her notebook, and my name, Lily, was off the list, just like that.

"I wouldn't want to go spend hours at some dumb wedding when I was half starving anyway. Everybody's going to faint before the dollar dance starts."

She stopped writing, "There isn't going to be a dollar dance." Then she wrinkled her wide nose, "Too gauche."

When I came back into the room after I had looked up the word, I told her, "I'm telling Mom you think she's tacky. You're carrying your gringa kick too far." Before shutting the bedroom door, I poked my head in and yelled, "I'm glad I'm not invited. I don't want to go to no white wedding."

Later, I asked her how she expected to go on her Hawaii honeymoon without a dollar dance. "You plan on selling the cucumber sandwiches at the wedding?"

She wiped the sarcastic smile off my face when she said, "No. I'm going to have a money tree." I told her that she was ridiculous and that she was going to be a laughingstock, not knowing how close my words were to the truth.

She didn't care what anyone thought. She said her wedding was hers, and it was one thing no one could ruin.

She kept up her lists as usual, but stopped physically adding to them in tenth grade—dropped and discarded as "too childish." By then, the lists were committed to memory, and I knew that she mentally scratched ex-friends and ex-boyfriends off of it. Lance, Rubén, Abraham, Artie, Oscar, Henry, Joel, and who knows who else had all been potential grooms.

It turned out to be Angel. He was beautiful, too—the Mexican version of the blond grooms in her magazines, right down to the cleft in his chin. He was perfect as long as he didn't smile, because when he smiled, his chipped, discolored front tooth showed. Rochelle worried about it all the time. She'd pull out photographs they had taken together, and the ones he had given her, to study them, trying to figure out the right camera angle that would hide his flaw. Anytime she mentioned getting it capped, he would roll his large almond-shaped eyes and smile. They would kiss and that would be the end of the discussion.

I knew this because Rochelle always had to drag me along on her dates. It was the only way our mother would allow her out of the house with a boy. I was a walking-and-talking birth control device. When we got home, I would replay the night's events for my mother. Funny, Ro relished the details of her wedding, but she never could stand for my instant replay of her dates. She would storm out of the living room when I would begin and slam the door to our bedroom. I usually had to sleep on the couch after our dates.

On prom night, Rochelle was allowed to go out with Angel alone, and she was so excited that she let me watch her dress for the big event. Tía Trini came over and rolled her hair, Prissy was there with her Tab in hand for moral support, and Mom was making last minute alterations to her gown. It was a salmon-colored version of her wedding dress. After she was teased, tweezed, and tucked, she looked like a stick of cotton candy from the top of her glittered hair down to her pink sling-back heels. When Angel saw her, he licked his lips like he was going to devour her.

Because I, her birth control device, wasn't in place during this date, the two got married when she was only a junior in high school, and she was four months pregnant. Rochelle and Angel drove thirty minutes to Las Cruces to be married by the justice of peace, with Mom in the back seat bawling. Even though Rochelle didn't get her elegant autumn wedding, she stood before Judge Grijalva in her off-white linen pantsuit, which was damp on the shoulder and smeared with Mom's mascara, erect and with as much dignity as if she were under a tent at the Chamizal. It didn't matter to her that the groom wore his blue Dickie work pants with matching shirt that had his name stitched in yellow onto the pocket. She looked at him like they were the only two people inside the closet-sized courtroom.

She didn't even blink when a baby began to wail in her ear during "Do you take this man . . ."

And she never took her eyes off Angel when the woman next in line to get married, who was dressed in a skin-tight, leopard-print outfit, said, "Let's get this show on the road already. Kiss her, kiss her already."

And it didn't bother Rochelle that after Angel kissed her, he looked at his watch and said, "Vámonos. I need to get back to work," because he needed to get back to Sears before the evening rush.

My Girlfriend Bobbi

I met Roberta Phillips my first day of high school. It was almost seven in the morning, and the sun wasn't up over the Franklins yet, so there was still a chill in the air. I wasn't wearing a coat, knowing that by mid-morning the sun would be high enough to give me a sunburn on the part in my hair. I sped up and watched my checkerboard Vans make dust clouds in the sand. When I stepped up onto the cement, I began to count. I counted to twenty-five before I bumped into Roberta Phillips and her dad.

"Careful, young man," Mr. Phillips said.

I looked up.

"She's a girl, Dad," Roberta said, turning to me and rolling her eyes at her father. "It's okay." Roberta picked up the purse I'd made her drop when I ran into her.

I stood there, grinning like a fool on her first date, and watched Roberta's father give her a hug and a kiss on the lips that lasted too long.

"You want to walk in together?" Roberta asked me, wiping his kiss off on her sleeve.

I nodded. "I'm sorry. I was looking down," I said, turning back to see her father watching us.

"Don't worry. I'm just glad I have somebody to walk inside with. My dad thinks anybody who wears pants is male. You're Patty, right? I get all freaked out on the first day of school. You can call me Bobbi. It's so much better than Roberta. Roberta makes me sound like a fat, dumpy girl. Anyway, it's like, even though I know everybody and everything, my stomach still does flips. First-day freakies, I guess."

I searched the hallways for anyone I knew who could rescue me, but the only person I saw was Lupe Cantú. I made a split-second decision—listen to what happened in Catechism last Sunday, or listen to the freakies. I turned to Bobbi, who was still talking.

"I know what everybody's thinking already. Oh, there goes the lesbian, and it's so not true."

"Everybody does not think that," I lied. "I don't."

"You're the only one."

Later, I found out it wasn't girls Bobbi liked—it was sex. Everything about her was sexual: her thick, red hair; her throaty, deep laugh; her dark, sad eyes; her sly, knowing smile. Even the freckles on her face were in a flirtatious pattern across the bridge of her nose, but it was her D-cup chest that made Bobbi so enticing to everyone. Girls stopped and stared with their mouths open in wonder. Her breasts were a sight to behold, and Bobbi let everyone get a good look. She was constantly touching, adjusting, and talking about them, like they were living, breathing, thinking beings. She even named them.

"Lisa and Clare here," she would say, touching Lisa, her left breast with a thick index finger that had dried blood around the nail in a crescent shape where she bit it, "were a hit last night. But poor Lisa is a little sore. Jimmy nibbled her when I finally let him touch her."

"You were with Jimmy Rodríguez?" I said. I usually said something like this because it amazed me how Bobbi always knew older guys, even guys out of school. And she would usually continue with something like. . .

"He's an idiot. I don't think he could tell you what color my eyes are. I got a good dinner out of him though."

A guy was the reason Bobbi and I became best friends. That and the fact that she saved my life. I was on my way to becoming Mrs. Anthony Vega. Anthony and I had dated an entire year, and he was already asking me if he could buy me a ring. Anthony was such a gentleman. He never once tried to unzip my pants or go up my shirt when we were making out in his car. I didn't think I could have found a better guy. Everybody at school just assumed we would marry and have children. He was so in love, and so was I, until one weekend in the bathroom line at a house party.

Bobbi stumbled into my back, and when I turned to see who it was, she fell into my arms.

"Oops," she giggled. "Patty, Patty Vega. Long time no see. You love Anthony, don't you? Don't you? I know something you don't."

"You're drunk, Bobbi," I said, lifting her away from me.

"Oh, God damn. Yes, I'm drunk. I bet you've never slept with little Tony." She put her hand in the air and wiggled her pinky.

"It's none of your business."

"Oh, shit. I'm right. How can you be with a guy for—what? Two years and not sleep with him? Are you stupid?"

"Shut up, damn it!"

"I'm sorry, Patty, I can't. Patty, your husband's dick is smaller than a, a Vienna sausage, and not even as thick."

A girl walked out of the bathroom. "You lying slut!" I said, then walked into the bathroom and slammed the door. Inside, I steadied myself on the tile counter and stared at my image long and hard. Bobbi had seen *a lot* of dicks. I must have been in the bathroom some time because a knock brought me back. I let the faucet run a few seconds, turned it off, and walked out the door. Bobbi was gone. I decided Anthony and I were going to have sex that night.

———

The next Monday at school, I skipped lunch and sat on the stadium bleachers by myself. I rested my head on my knees. I heard a clang on the aluminum benches and saw the busty redhead hiking toward me. She talked as she stepped.

"Patty. I'm sorry. I'm so sorry. I was wrong. What I said was so wrong. I was drunk. I heard you and Anthony broke up. And I'd feel awful if it was because of what I said. It's just that sometimes I get so mean when I'm drunk. I'm just an insecure bitch. I'm jealous. You and Anthony have true love. I'm so sorry." She sat two seats below me and looked up.

"It's okay," I said.

She was quiet.

"You were right."

"No, no, I'm wrong."

"It is small," I lifted my pinky and wiggled it. "And I'm shallow."
I put my head back on my knees and wept.

"Shhh. Shhh. You're not shallow. Don't say that."

"Yes—," I sobbed, and then snorted, "I . . . am. I checked. After
you said what you said. I checked. I wanted to see for myself. I had
to see for myself. I wondered why he never wanted to do more
than kiss. Now I know."

She hugged me until I stopped crying. When I had finished,
she placed her hands on my cheeks. My heart pounded because I
thought she was going to kiss me, but she simply raised my head,
looked me in the eyes, and absolved me of my sin.

She said, "Sex is a very important part of a relationship, and a
girl should know exactly what she is getting herself into."

I looked at her in disbelief, and realized we were both very
much alike. After that day we were inseparable.

I thought it was funny that she, of all people, got labeled a
lesbian. When I asked her about it, she told me it all started in
junior high. When she refused to kiss Steven Archuleta, he called
her a lesbian. It was a stupid thing for her to do because everyone
absolutely loved the guy, including me. But Bobbi told me that
she got it in her head that playing hard to get was the way to go
with this one. I saw it differently. If there was one thing Bobbi
knew, it was guys. She knew what she wanted from them and
how to get it, but it was the other stuff she had a hard time with.
Something as simple as "Do you want a Coke or some milk with your
sandwich?" confused her. It got so I just stopped asking, gave her
what I was drinking, and she was fine. Relieved. I'm sure Lupe
Cantú, her best friend in junior high, had a lot to do with it.
Lupita was a Holy Roller, the only girl in public school who wore a
uniform. She carried the Bible with her everywhere she went, even
PE, and she loved Ash Wednesdays. All the teachers thought she
was such a good Catholic girl because she didn't wipe the ashes
off of her forehead, like everyone else did, but kept them there just
to show how close she was to God. What the teachers didn't see
was their Lupita in art class with her nose so far down a rubber
cement bottle that the hairs in her nose shined. I should have known
then that Lupe would be a sniffer. I guess the Bible didn't mention
inhalants, because Lupita dropped out of school in eleventh

grade after she was banned from art class. Every time I saw her hanging on the street, she had a silver ring around her mouth and nose. And she was skinny. She was skinny like the models in the magazines we were all trying to be like, only nobody envied her. I think Lupita's Bible stories got Bobbi all mixed up, and poor Steven never got his kiss.

Bobbi also told me that the one good thing about everyone thinking she was lesbian was the guys. Football and basketball players were always trying to convert her. She had her pick. They wanted to show her what real men were like, and she let them. She even let their coaches try to convert her. The high-school boys' basketball coach was one of the youngest coaches in the district, tall and handsome. All the girls had a crush on him, including Bobbi. And this man liked the high school girls right back. He liked them so much he would get them out of class to meet in his office inside the gym. That was where I found coach and Bobbi. She had her muscular gymnast's legs wrapped around his waist when I walked in to give him the roll sheet he'd asked for at the front office. They both laughed at me when Bobbi motioned me to come toward them, and I stepped back. Then they went right on doing what they were doing before I came in. I closed the door and shook my head, wondering if all athletic coaches were made from the same batch. The girls' volleyball coach was just as bad, only she was a woman. She'd invite the volleyball team over to her apartment, and they'd play strip poker. She kept inviting me even though I wasn't on the team. I guess she hadn't heard that it was Bobbi, and not me, who swung that way.

While Bobbi got dates every weekend, I sat at home and watched cable television. Our friend Calvin would drop by when he didn't have a date, and sometimes Max would stop in. The two would smoke pot, while I made quesadillas for their munchies. Max would try to teach Calvin Spanish—telling him things like joto meant good looking. I felt bad for Calvin, not because he was the only black guy at our high school, but because he was the most girlie guy, and he couldn't help it. Being different in high school was rough enough, but being flagrantly feminine was unforgivable. All the stupid jerks on the football team took every opportunity to body slam Calvin into lockers. They thought it was hilarious to watch him drop his books on the floor every period. Calvin was good about it, too. He'd say, "It's cool, bro. We're cool," while those thick-necked jerks would chuckle and say something stupid, like "Yeah, you bet your ass we're cool." I would have probably cried getting slammed into the lockers every day. Not Calvin; he took it all in stride, or so I thought.

The first day of our senior year, Calvin, Bobbi, and I were walking down the hall, talking about how this was going to be our year and planning our futures. Calvin was talking in his high voice, gesturing wildly with his one free hand like he did, and telling us how, now that he was a senior, nobody was going to bother him. Bobbi said she was going to try out for the university cheerleading squad because she could do backflips. She hadn't thought about the fact that she hadn't passed freshman English. Still, she was telling us how being a cheerleader in college wasn't a popularity contest like in high school, when we saw Sam Delgado.

Sam was your typical fat-necked, Mexican macho teenager. His father had two families, one in El Paso and the other across the river in Juárez. I knew this because Sandra Castillo told me. She and Sam's older sister were tight, and apparently Sam's sister talked about "the bitches on the other side" all the time. She also hated her brother, who was the only boy in either family, which meant Sam was spoiled rotten and favored like he was some kind of king or something. I knew Sam was going to knock Calvin into the lockers even before Sam knew it. The big oaf was walking toward us with his pack of friends and those Mexican girls who insisted they were Spanish, and he wasn't about to let an opportunity to show off pass him by.

What Calvin did after he was body slammed was a thing of beauty. It made me so happy I cried. In fact, it was the high point of my high school career, and probably his, too. As the pack was laughing, pointing, and carrying on, Calvin bent down to pick up his books, and when he looked up, he had tears in his eyes, real tears. Then he said, "Sam, what happened? I thought you liked my blow jobs." There was maybe five seconds of silence before Bobbi roared with laughter, and I watched as Sam's silent pack tried to stifle theirs. One girl giggled, then a boy, and then another, until the entire crowd was laughing so hard tears formed in their eyes.

And Sam was livid. Droplets of sweat formed above his upper lip, and I thought he was going to kick the shit out of Calvin right then and there, but he didn't. He was too embarrassed. So he walked away, which made me think, maybe Calvin did give Sam blow jobs. Everyone else must have been thinking that, too, because another roar came from the pack. Calvin was right; no one ever bothered him again during his senior year.

I only wished Bobbi could do something like that to get rid of her father. Bobbi was the only person I knew whose life was more screwed up than Calvin's. Her father liked to do it with her. Calvin said that was why Bobbi was so promiscuous. Bobbi started to cry when I told her what he had said because she thought it was a bad word. When I told her that promiscuous meant she slept with a lot of guys, she wiped the tears from her eyes and said, "Oh, well, yeah. I thought it meant Calvin didn't like me."

Her dad was always creeping around us when I'd go and visit. He was a tall white man with curly red hair, and I would have considered him handsome if I didn't already know him. He looked like a little boy. His front teeth had a gap so wide it looked like a tooth was missing, and to this day I still associate gap-toothed men with child molesters. Sometimes when I slept over, I'd wake up in the middle of the night, and he'd be in our room, lying in Bobbi's bed with her. Her mother acted like he was the best husband in the world. He was real nice to everyone, and he never bothered me except for the times when he'd walk into Bobbi's bedroom without knocking and do things like slap her on the butt, caress her shoulder-length hair, or wipe food from her mouth when she was eating. Whenever I ate dinner with the Phillips, Bobbi always tried to sit across from her father, but he insisted she sit next to him. He would make her get up and move over. Bobbi's mom, Connie, would talk a mile a minute in Spanish, thrilled to have someone who understood her, while ignoring her daughter's protests and her husband's greedy eyes. Once, when I dropped my napkin and bent down to get it, I noticed that Mr. Phillips was fondling Bobbi under the table. I was amazed at how calm and collected they both were, and how stupid I was not to know what was going on. Ever since then I stopped eating dinner with them. The whole thing made me kind of sick, to tell the truth. But I didn't blame Bobbi for being promiscuous. I'd have been, too, if I had a father who did what hers did.

My mother nearly pulled off a chunk of my hair that she was braiding when I told her about Bobbi's father.

"Don't ever go to that house again. Do you hear me, Patty? If I ever caught anyone doing that—Oh God, I don't even want to think about it. Death. Death. That's what that man deserves. ¿Y la mamá? ¿Es mexicana, qué no? And she's letting this happen in her own house?"

When I saw the tears in her eyes, I promised her I would never spend the night there again. It actually worked out pretty good for me because Mom never asked any questions whenever Bobbi spent the night. It got so she was living with us during the school months, and I enjoyed cuddling up next to Bobbi in my twin bed. She was always so warm. Our night-time routine was to shower, get dressed for bed, listen to a few records, turn out the lights, and talk in bed until we couldn't see straight. When Bobbi turned her back to me in bed, I would put my arm around her waist, and wait. Sometimes she would lift my hand to her breast, and we would fool around, and sometimes we would just go to sleep.

Comfort

When Courtney took the cereal box out of the cupboard, she felt Eliseo's eyes on her. She heard him sigh, and it angered her. It was a sound she had heard a million times before, she thought. Courtney turned her head to face him. Eliseo sat hunched over a neatly inscribed ledger. His husky frame dwarfed the wooden folding chair he sat in at the kitchen table. A calculator and a book lay open before him. He was half-dressed in boxer shorts and a pink oxford shirt, stained with the day's sweat. His massive arm cuddled the ledger, while his left hand tapped a beat with a pencil on the table top. He looked up at her with those dark eyes, always seeming on the verge of tears. She blinked and turned her head back toward her bowl. Then she heard the words that set her off.

"You can't eat cereal at night," Eliseo chastised her.

"Just watch me!" she said, once again turning toward him, as she shoved a spoonful of oats into her mouth like a starving child. Milk slopped down her chin, dripped onto the kitchen counter, and then dribbled to the floor. She chewed with her mouth open, the cereal cracking. She didn't bother to wipe the milk off her face. He was always setting limits. He limited his eating, drinking, and even his television time. Courtney was the exact opposite. She gorged herself on food, drink, or entertainment. Her appetites were as big as his muscles. She thought they made an odd couple: Eliseo, with his Mr. Universe physique, and she, a petite, doughy figure on his arm. He had rules and methods—systematic ways to save money, make money, eat, sleep, make love, control her life—always so practical.

"We can do anything we want, Eliseo. We can drink coffee at

night, piss in the shower, and even, even eat breakfast at night! We make the rules!"

"No, you can't. The carbs in the cereal are going to make you sleepy, babe," he said, frowning while staring at her T-shirt. "You'll be sluggish in the morning, and your energy level will be nil. All that sugar messes with your sleep."

She slammed the cereal bowl inside the chipped porcelain sink. "I don't give a rat's ass!"

"I'm just warning you," he said quietly.

He couldn't leave well enough alone. Why couldn't he just shut up? Courtney thought Eliseo's brooding eyes looked sad, or maybe angry, because she wore an old lover's white T-shirt, which read "Sunland Park—Where the Action Is!" She knew he hated the shirt.

Eliseo furrowed his brow. "I'm not him."

"I know," Courtney whispered.

"Why do you have to wear it?" Eliseo looked at the shirt.

"It's just a fucking shirt." She poked her fist through the hole near the hem.

He sighed.

"It's over," Courtney turned to walk out of the kitchen, but her foot slid on the milky floor, and she fell. She sat Indian style where she had landed.

Eliseo stood but she waved him away. When she stepped out of her sitting position to stand, her toe caught the hole in the shirt, and when she stood, it tore in a circle around her body.

Eliseo smiled, then quickly covered his mouth with his hand.

Standing, Courtney said, "Stop hiding shit. If you feel something then feel it, for Christ's sake."

Charlie would have never let her get away with talking to him like that. She didn't remember what would set Charlie off, why or how she would hit the floor, only that she was there.

Eliseo shut the open book on the table, and Courtney knew he was asking, "What's wrong?" She wouldn't play along today. His wounded look when she didn't answer annoyed her. Those moist, dark eyes she had found so charming when they first met only frustrated her now. He shed tears too easily. He was nothing like Charlie.

Charlie's pointed-toe boots always found the softest spots on her body. That's how Eliseo had found out about him. He saw the bruises, and she couldn't keep her stories straight. One evening, after a particularly bad afternoon with Charlie, she'd told Eliseo she had fallen down some steps, and the next morning, she had said she had tripped in the park. Eliseo had asked her to stop seeing him. She agreed because she knew Charlie was never going to leave his wife. She had tried cheating on him, but he'd only beat her more, then go back to his wife. Like the time he'd caught her in the freezer with Jimmy in the back of Club 101. Her ass had been freezing and numb by the time Charlie walked in and found them. Then there were the times she didn't deserve it. Like the time she had asked the waiter to repeat the dinner specials. Charlie had got up, led her out of the restaurant, and slapped her. *He* was doing the ordering, he said.

"Maybe I should knock the shit out of you, too," Eliseo's eyes watered.

Courtney stood, unsure if she had spoken, then said, "Just try it."

Eliseo would never hit a woman. The worst those heavy, muscled arms had done to Courtney was cut off her circulation whenever he rested them on top of her in bed at night.

Respect. Something every girl wanted but didn't really need. What Courtney wanted was passion. At 22, Courtney felt a bit cheated. She longed for someone like Charlie, or even a relationship like that of her best friend, Eva, and her boyfriend, Tony.

Eva had been wired the night Tony walked right up to her at the Mexican dance club, GeeGee's. He had grabbed her, like he owned her, right on the dance floor, while she had been dancing with another man. Courtney had felt turned on. Courtney and Eliseo had watched as Eva twisted her skinny arm away from Tony's grip. He'd made a stab for it again but had caught her partner's forearm instead. The short, stocky, barrel-chested man Eva was with had taken a swing and his fist had landed on Tony's temple and Tony had fallen. Eva had jumped on the man's back and had sunk her teeth into the nape of his neck. He had yelled and flipped her right off.

Eva lay on the floor with her pink miniskirt up over her hips so that her black lace panties had shown, and her orangutan-orange–colored hair had glowed green and red from the lights un–derneath the dance floor. Enraged, Tony had charged like a young bull toward the man, who was trying to walk away from the crowd of dancers. Impatient, Eliseo had wrapped his hand completely around Courtney's bicep and then jerked her to get her to move toward the door. He'd used more force than she had thought he would ever use on her, and her muscles tightened. Once out of the dance club, they'd heard sirens, and they ran for two blocks before Eliseo had flagged down a taxi to get them over to the American side. Courtney had sat flushed next to Eliseo.

He'd said, "The Mexican jails are rough for Americans," in that same calm voice he used to tell her that the cereal's carbohydrates would make her sluggish.

His explanation had been met with silence.

Courtney reasoned that Eliseo was a good and decent man. He was smart, too. He ate right, jogged a little, and lifted weights every day, rain or shine. No matter how hard she had tried to get him to stay in bed with her all day, he always lifted. Said he needed his release. It was refreshing to hear, in a way, because all of Courtney's other boyfriends got their release on top of her. Then, she realized Eliseo really did need the release. He needed it because he was a coward. He never wanted to argue; he wanted to discuss things. Discuss. Anytime she raised her voice, he would excuse himself, telling her she needed to be alone until she had calmed down. After she was calm, they could discuss any problem she had, he'd said. Discuss. She wanted to beat on his chest, but he gave her absolutely no reason. He would leave, and she would stew. Stew all alone, cry, and finally, fall asleep. It was when she was sleeping that Eliseo would sneak in and hold her until she woke. He never wanted to face anything when it needed to be faced.

What she needed was someone more like Tony or Charlie. Someone who would, when angry, slam his fist in the wall next to her head to show her that he loved her so much that he couldn't control himself. Courtney's father loved her mother that much. After nights out, they would come home and he would smash holes in walls, angry that her mother had flirted with his friends. Those nights, loud and violent, ended with soft and frenzied moaning in their bedroom. On those nights, no one else in the house mattered.

And Courtney, who sat on the floor in the hallway, her cheek red from being pressed to the door, was comforted by those nights.

But Eliseo was all about control. Jesus, even his climaxes were controlled. His soft, stilted "Oh, Courtney" made her skin crawl. Right before he came, he would grab her shoulders hard enough to leave red blotches on her white skin. She would smile and want him to lose control, but then he would loosen his grip. Afraid to hurt her, afraid of intensity, afraid of life itself, it seemed. He would stop himself. He wanted to know how she felt. Could she come?

Could she come? Of course she could, and when she did, she didn't give a shit about him. It was all about her, and when and how intense it was going to be. Jesus, could she come? Just once, Courtney would like to go to bed with him and have him not ask her that question. Not care what the fuck she was feeling and just satisfy himself without giving her a thought. Most men did. What was he trying to prove?

Eliseo picked up his ledger from the table, stood, and said, "You need to be alone."

"Alone. That's the last thing I need right now, Eliseo—the last thing. But then, what would you know about what a woman needs. You don't even know how to fuck."

Courtney saw that Eliseo's eyes were tearing up for real now. The fuck comment had hit its mark. Despite his size, he had the temperament of a frightened schoolboy. He had always said that he couldn't believe she was interested in him. Still couldn't believe it. Which might explain why he was so cautious. He hadn't figured out it was caution that got a person axed from a relationship.

"Why did you say that?" His wide brown face was red and looked like it would implode.

"Because *you* don't know how to fuck, and you're a bore. The biggest bore I've ever met," she said, unable to stop the words. "I don't understand how you don't put yourself to sleep when you talk."

The tears that puddled in his dark eyes began to flow down his cheeks. Courtney looked down at her bare feet and noticed that the nail polish on the big toe was chipped. She made a mental note to paint it later. When she looked up again, Eliseo's face was purple. She frowned, and he stood up quickly. She backed up against the

cupboard. The pencil between his fingers snapped in two; Courtney didn't see it, but she heard it. His intensity and silence made
her laugh out loud. Eliseo's watering eyes locked on her face, and
he took a step toward her. She realized he wasn't the stupid boy
she had believed him to be.

Eliseo grabbed hold of both of Courtney's white arms. His large
hands wrapped completely around her biceps, just like at GeeGee's.
He was squeezing her too tight, and before she could complain, he
shoved her.

She flew backward into the wooden cupboard door. The metal
doorknob dug into her back and tore her flesh. The impact knocked
the wind out of her, and she laughed through fits of coughing.
Eliseo moved toward her again with his large hand balled into a
fist. That fist hit her on the right side of the jaw like a knock with
a sack of rocks. The left side of her face slammed against the white
cupboard. She lost her balance and slid, slid down the cupboard.
When her butt hit the floor, she fell to her side.

Specks of red littered the yellow floor. The specks were blood.
Her blood. She was bleeding from her nose. She could feel it now,
flowing down onto her mouth.

Eliseo kicked her. She doubled over in pain. Blows of pain hit
her ribs, arms, and legs. She was thankful that he was barefoot. She
tried to sit up but couldn't. She screamed.

"Eliseo! Eliseo stop!"

He stood over her. The tears on his cheeks were now only dirty
lines on his face. He was looking down at her but didn't see her.
Instead of helping her up, he turned around, picked up the broken
pencil on the floor, and walked out of the room.

Courtney felt hot and flushed. He just left her there on the
floor with her T-shirt covered in blood. She grasped the cupboard
door handle and lifted herself to her feet. She stumbled. She heard
Eliseo banging around in the other room, slamming drawers. At
the kitchen sink, she turned on the water faucet. She caught the
cold water in her cupped hand, then cleaned the blood from her
face. She watched the water swirling crimson and pink down the
drain. The more blood she saw, the bigger she smiled. She wanted
to go to Eliseo to tell him that she loved him, and that she didn't
mean a thing she had said.

When she turned away from the sink, her jaw came to life. It throbbed. She opened and closed her mouth wide, squinted back tears, then she smiled again.

Eliseo walked into the room dressed, clutching his briefcase. He didn't look at her when he opened the kitchen door. As he stepped through the doorway he coolly inspected the damage to her face. It was the first time Eliseo had looked at Courtney without the softness of tears. Courtney felt sad and sorry. But when he closed the door, she stood alone, smiling.

Goldfinger

I was eleven, Aaron was thirteen, Danny was eight, and Bobby was seventeen when we crossed the freeway from south El Paso to the good side of town. Dad wanted to move to the eastside to get away from the south-side cholos. He was afraid we'd all end up in prison or maimed from a gang fight. So he worked all the time to make enough money to pay for our new house and cable TV. We left behind our friends and family. We never saw Bobby, probably because he spent his time driving around the old neighborhood while we chased lizards into tumbleweeds. The square, light-brown house we lived in looked like every other house on our block. The only reason we didn't walk into somebody else's place by mistake was because ours was last on the five-house street. Our next door neighbors to the east were tumbleweeds and sand as far as you could see. The boxy house we lived in had two windows out front, a garage with two doors, and a front door with rectangular glass windows on either side. Over here, there was no Señora Monsiváis, whose Pepto-Bismol-pink colored house was hard to see because of the rows of sunflowers and corn in her front yard. Instead of grass or gardens out front, everyone on the east side had landscaping rocks. Kids played inside. We couldn't stand being inside because the house smelled like paint, new carpet, and wood that had just been cut. The old house on the other side of the freeway smelled like chile colorado, old pillows, and Raid. Because of Aaron, we had to stay inside the weird smelling house a lot.

One time he threw a cascarón with used motor oil at Clarissa Dobsin's puffy blue Easter dress. It had been a regular day for us that could have ended worse than it did, if it hadn't been for Aaron. "She should know better," Aaron said as he poured used motor oil from a coffee can sitting in our front yard into the hole of the hollow egg. The pretty, blonde-haired girl was always wearing her good clothes and playing in them outside. Clarissa got it right on her flat chest. The idiot didn't even move. She looked like someone had shot her in the heart. We all laughed as she cried. Then we ran inside the house, praying she wouldn't tell.

Inside the den, I pulled on the silver-coated plastic knob to turn on the Zenith. The black set buzzed and a horizontal white line across the screen appeared, then separated, and we saw two old farts sitting in uncomfortable chairs talking about Jesus Christ.

"Jenny, do you think *Goldfinger* is on?" Danny asked.

I stood in front of the television set, looking down on the brown and tan cable box that had all the stations we could ever want, even the nasty ones that showed porno movies. At the old house, we only had three channels, not including the Sesame Street one.

"I'm positive. It only comes on a hundred times a day." I noticed Aaron was quiet, watching Danny's hamster, Ben.

Ben's home was inside an aquarium in front of our brick fireplace. It had a steel exercise wheel inside. The rectangular glass tank used to hold Danny's fish, but Aaron killed them off by putting Clorox in the water as an experiment. Danny and I walked over to where Aaron was standing and watched as Ben clutched a green and white ball between his little hand-like paws. Every so often, he would take a bite of the ball and chew it, like he was eating pan de huevo from Bowie Bakery. His black unblinking eyes stared back at us.

"What's he eating?" Danny asked Aaron, touching the aquarium glass with his index finger.

"What's it look like?" Aaron rubbed his shiny nose.

We said, "I dunno," shrugging our shoulders, sweat dripping from the sides of our faces onto our matching thin, blue Superman T-shirts.

"Look hard," Aaron said, as he placed his index finger inside his right nostril and laughed.

As Ben chewed and Aaron rubbed his nose, it hit me.

"You gross pig!" I spit up my laughter.

"What? What? What's he eating, Jenny?"

"It's a booger," I laughed, running my hand over Danny's bald head. Dad always took him to Juárez to get a buzz, and Rubén's haircuts made Danny look like one of those concentration camp victims we saw in *Life* magazine at the library. The fact that he was as skinny as the new mulberry trees in our backyard added to the effect. Rubén gave all kids a boot–camp haircut, even girls. I got one once. Mom wouldn't talk to Dad until my hair grew out long enough to where you didn't see my white head.

"Will it hurt him?" Danny said, tilting his head like a puppy. He always looked that way when he was concerned.

"I wanted to see if Ben thought boogers were salty," Aaron answered, using his mock scientist voice. It was the same serious tone he used to calm Danny when he was conducting an experiment.

The three of us watched as Ben, who was named after a Jackson Five song we all liked, finished off the booger. When he was done, he sniffed at his paws to make sure he really was finished, and he headed straight for his water tube.

Aaron looked triumphant. His smile flashed his block straight teeth. His big belly shook as he giggled until tears came to his eyes. The familiar sight always made us laugh. The unscientific experiments he conducted passed the time between three and seven, when Mom would pull up from work, and Dad would get home with groceries from the Rainbow Bread Day Old Store and the WIC downtown.

Aaron took a running leap from where he stood by Ben's aquarium and landed on our brown vinyl couch. He didn't stick to the sofa because he was wet with sweat. We all were. The cooler wasn't working, and we could hear its constant hum. Aaron wiped his shiny face on the pillows he was hugging. He hogged all five and wouldn't give us one to share. Danny lay in front of the TV, facing the screen, and propped his head up with his hands resting on his elbows. I stood over the brown box, trying to remember the "007" channel.

"It's number 39, dummy," Aaron said from the couch.

I punched down the rectangular tan button numbered 39, and sure enough, Sean Connery was just waking up from the poison dart shot at him. Pussy Galore was there to meet him. I dove next to Danny and propped my head up with my hands, too.

Aaron laughed when Pussy Galore introduced herself. It wasn't long before we heard the familiar crackle of vinyl, and Aaron was gone. Danny and I both crawled over to the couch and grabbed two pillows each, leaving Aaron only one.

We were watching the scene unfolding on the screen in front of us when we heard Aaron running down the hall, trying to mimic Shirley Bassey's voice, "Goldfinger. He's the man, the man with the caca touch."

Before I could look up, he was on top of me. I felt his knees on my skinny arms and his butt on my back. I couldn't move an inch. All I could do was bob my head from side to side and slap him with my hair. When Aaron grabbed a mess of hair on top of my head and pulled my face upward, I watched as 007 was locked into a cell.

"You fucker," I yelled, with my head up, eyes looking at the acoustic ceiling.

Aaron's hysterical laughter worried me. I saw his index finger going for my throat but instead of poking me, he put the append-age directly under my nose and slashed upwards like someone cutting somebody's throat. My eyes watered and my nostrils flared as I inhaled the damp, musky, shit odor on his finger.

I screamed at the ceiling, "You fucking retard!"

As quickly as he hit, he was gone. I heard him singing "Gold-finger" again and then a thump in the direction of the hallway, and I knew Danny hadn't made it into his room. By the time I reached him in the hall, Aaron had already run into the bathroom, shut the door, and locked it.

"You sick, Mongoloid, fat-ass fucker," I yelled, banging on the outside of the hollow wooden door.

"Yeah, you, you, you, booger-feeding hamster gross head," Danny yelled, his face red.

We heard the water from the faucet running and Aaron's laugh-ter. Unable to get in, we went back to watch *Goldfinger* and didn't talk to Aaron for at least twenty minutes.

We knew when Mom got home from work because our station wagon died with a bang whenever it came to a stop. The three of us heard it, and ran into Aaron's bedroom, stepped onto the mat-tress on the floor, and peeked between the white bed sheets Mom had tacked to the window as curtains. We could see her in the car getting her purse from the passenger seat and she looked tired, like always. She adjusted the rearview mirror in front of her and was still when she noticed Mrs. Dobsin walking up the driveway. Mom watched the stiff-legged woman through the rearview mirror before she opened the car door. When she stepped out of the car, Mrs. Dobsin was standing in front of her.

"Mrs. Ar . . . , Mrs., Mrs. Archy Leta," was how she pronounced Mom's name. She sounded like her mouth hurt. "We have a serious problem."

"Oh?" was what Mom said before Mrs. Dobsin began.

"Your children. Well, they have no supervision between the time school lets out and when you get home." She crossed her arms tightly to her chest, and just her mouth moved when she spoke. "They really shouldn't be home alone. I mean, you should be home with your children. They need their mother."

Mom spoke to Mrs. Dobsin like she was talking to a bill collector. Whenever bill collectors called on the telephone, Mom talked to them in a soft, high voice. She sounded like the Brady Bunch Mom, and she wouldn't say anything in Spanish. "Don't you think, Mrs. Dobsin," Mom said, emphasis on—sin, "that I would be home with my children if we could afford it?" She pointed down the street as she said, "Do you think I'm working two shifts at the clinic because I enjoy my work?" She brought her fist to her chest, her head bobbed up and down, "I'm sorry, but I don't have that luxury."

Mrs. Dobsin took one step away from Mom, who was at least four inches shorter than she was and said, "Oh, well, I didn't mean to . . . I mean . . . " She tightened her blonde pony tail. "Well, why I came is because . . . I'm here because, Clarissa. Her dress is ruined."

"What happened?" Mom's voice came out low and still.

"Your children threw an egg at her. It was filled with oil. Now her dress, the brand new dress we bought her for Easter, is ruined. I can't get the stain out."

"It was *my* kids that did it?"

"They're the only other children on the block."

"I'll take care of them, and we'll buy Clarissa a new dress."

"Oh, no, you don't need to do that . . . " Mrs. Dobsin began, but something in my Mom's face made her stop.

From the window, all I saw was Mom's black hair tied in a Aqua Net tight bun, the back of her red, wrinkled blouse, which had a dark circle of sweat, and her blue skirt that sagged around the butt.

Mrs. Dobsin, who looked rested in her faded jeans and starched, pink cotton shirt, asked while taking another step back, "Could you please tell your son to stop harassing her?"

Aaron yelled from the window, "I didn't touch her ass!"

Both women looked toward the house, and the three of us fell back and lay flat away from Mom's "I'm–going–to–beat–you" glare. We knew Aaron was going to die, especially if Mom was mad enough to tell Dad. Mom apologized and said goodbye to Mrs. Dobsin. We heard Mom's shoes on the cement driveway and the front door open. Mom opened the bedroom door, stepped inside, then closed it behind her, even though we were the only ones in the house. She still had her greasy lunch bag and purse in one hand.

"What the hell are you kids trying to do to me? Why can't you just be normal children, like, like Clarissa?" Mom's sweat mustache dripped onto her lips. "What's wrong with you Aaron? Are you retarded?"

When Aaron interrupted with "Mom, you don't—," she flipped out and raised the empty hand to hit Aaron but instead pointed her finger toward all of us, "Shut up! And get out of my face. I don't even want to see your asses until your Dad gets home."

We waited. We heard the loud slam of the car door. Aaron, who was at the window, ran out of the room to the front door to let Dad inside. Sometimes we joked around with Dad if everything went okay at work, but most of the time, he was pissed off. Anything we said would set him off. We could tell it was one of those days when he slammed the heavy door of his silver Buick shut.

"It's hot as hell in here! Didn't you idiots turn on the cooler?" was the first thing Dad said when he stepped inside.

"Yes sir, it's on," Aaron said, muscles tightened.

"Goddamn it. It's always something," Dad said, dropping the two paper sacks he held in one arm onto the dining room table. He was forever fixing things at the new house. His large forearms were all I saw when he pointed to Aaron then up at the ceiling. "Get up there and check and see if the deals are wet."

Aaron looked at us, and we at him, shrugging our shoulders. Mom walked into the dining room from the kitchen holding a spatula. She raised her thin, black eyebrows, then squinted at Danny and me to keep quiet. She looked at Aaron.

"I think your Dad wants you to check to make sure the pads are getting water," Mom said. "Whew, hace mucho calor. How did you stand it in here? Why didn't you go outside?"

"Cause this place sucks, remember?" Aaron said, rolling his eyes as he walked past Dad toward the back door in the kitchen.

"Don't even talk to your mother that way," Dad slapped Aaron on the back of the head as he walked in front of him.

Aaron's shiny blue–black hair shook from the impact. Ears red, his answer was a stiff, "Yes sir," as he continued walking.

Mom nodded her head and turned to us. "Okay, help me put away the groceries."

I unloaded cans with white labels onto empty shelves and glanced at Mom's profile by the stove. The one eye I saw stared straight ahead into the wall as she stirred a pot of boiling beans. I wondered if she was thinking about telling Dad about Aaron. Before I could ask her, Danny pulled my arm, and we walked through the back door and outside to watch Aaron, who was already on the roof. As the smell of boiling beans hung in the hot air, Aaron undid the screws on the sheet metal that boxed our swamp cooler. I heard the metal crash on the shingles.

Danny and I giggled because we knew that Aaron, like an idiot, had forgotten that the metal was hot. He stood up, looked down at us, shook his hips, waved his index finger, and mouthed, "Goldfinger." Danny and I laughed because it was like watching a smaller, fatter version of Dad shaking it on the roof. I gave him the finger.

Aaron looked inside the cooler and placed his hand between the pulley and the motor that was connected to the blower. He shifted his weight to get a better look inside, and all I saw was his broad back and the back of his head. Then I heard him scream.

He was on the roof holding his bloody right hand at the wrist with his left hand. Danny ran into the house, repeating Aaron's name over and over.

"What is it now?" Dad's voice turned from anger to horror, ¿Qué pasó?" He charged out the screened, wooden back door. "Fuck!" he said with wild eyes, as his lean body took the ladder steps in twos. He did not notice how hot the ladder was to the touch.

When Dad got his footing on the roof, he stripped off his T-shirt and wrapped it around Aaron's bloody hand. He led Aaron down the hot ladder to where Mom was standing, reaching up for him. The T-shirt was completely red. Dad lifted him out of Mom's grip, then ran with Aaron in his arms through the back door, into the house, then back out the front door and into the car.

Mom grabbed the keys to the Buick and followed them. She drove in reverse out of the driveway and shouted, "Watch the beans, and turn off the meat! We'll call you from the hospital!"

Danny was crying as I rubbed his head. I led him back toward the kitchen, where I stirred the beans and turned the gas burner cooking the ground beef to off. Danny tugged the hem on the back of my T-shirt. I dragged him across the linoleum kitchen floor, from the stove into the den, like the jet skiers we saw on TV. We sat in the den and watched Ben sleep. The woman on TV, who was on all fours like a dog, lifting her leg high into the air behind her, hypnotized us.

Fifteen minutes later, we heard Bobby's car in the driveway. When he walked into the house, he said, "It's hot as hell in here." Then the phone rang, and he answered it.

"Yeah," Bobby said, standing in the kitchen doorway, eyeing the woman in leotards on TV. From the floor, I looked up and saw his black, bushy eyebrows become one as he concentrated on the information he was being given from the other end. The person on the line was giving him instructions. I knew because he was nodding his head up and down, the way he did whenever Dad explained something to him.

When Bobby got off the phone, he headed for the fridge. Danny and I followed him. He took all five of the ice cube trays out of the freezer and popped ice cubes onto the tile counter. He opened several cabinet doors until he found the white box with the plastic sandwich baggies. He took one out and dropped six ice cubes into the bag; then he ran out into the backyard and climbed the ladder. He screamed for me to turn off the cooler from inside, which I did.

When he came back down, he said, "Mom told me to get Aaron's finger out of the reservoir and bring it to them at the hospital."

Danny began to cry again, and Bobby put the bag with Aaron's finger behind his back so we couldn't see it. The ice cubes on the counter were already half their regular size and water dripped onto the floor. Bobby ran out of the kitchen as I rubbed Danny's head and watched the drips.

———————

Aaron didn't come home for three days, and when he did, his whole hand looked five times its normal size. Mom told us they couldn't put his finger back on because it had fallen into the reservoir water, which was filled with rust, bugs, and dirt.

"So Aaron doesn't have his finger, his gold finger?" Danny asked.

"Yes, he's going to be missing his finger," Mom told us. "I want you two to be extra nice to him. You can't go fooling around like you normally do, at least not until it heals. The doctor said Aaron might be different now."

"Different how?" I wanted to know.

"He might be mad about losing his finger or he might just be sad all the time," Mom said. "The doctor said he might not want to get out of bed for a while, and he might not want to eat."

"I know how he feels," Danny said. "I felt that way every time I lost one of my fish. It was like I lost a part of me, and I was so sad."

"Yeah, right, Daniel, that's exactly what your big brother will feel like," Mom said. "You two be nice to him and try to help. He's going to need all of us."

Mom didn't go to work the rest of the week, and we got to stay home from school. All we did was watch TV and wonder if Aaron would ever be the same. Mom let us inside his room on the second day he was home.

His face was the color of Dad's pale stomach. The swelling in his hand had gone down. It was still big, the size of Dad's hand. Mom told us not bother him, so we stayed on the floor and watched his chest go up and down. After a few minutes, he opened his eyes. Danny and I sat on our knees and leaned in toward Aaron to get a better look at his face. He blinked once, twice, and frowned.

"Does your hand hurt?" Danny asked.

I elbowed him in the ear.

"Ay, that hurt," Danny said, rubbing the side of his head.

Aaron gave us a sleepy smile that was too nice coming from him.

"It hurts like hell until Mom gives me those blue pills," Aaron said, in a whisper.

"Do you want one now?" Danny asked.

"Nah."

"What did they do with your finger?" Danny said.

And again I elbowed him on the head.

Aaron looked at both of us, then at his wrapped hand lying on top of two pillows. With his good hand, he waved for us to come closer to him. Hypnotized, we crawled closer to the bed so that we were face to face.

Then he said, "They sewed it back on to my hand."

"Mom said they couldn't . . . Ay!" Danny said.

"They sewed it back on. At first, they didn't think they could, but some redheaded English dude came into the operation room and said he could do it. Before they knocked me out, I asked him if he could sew it onto my palm." Aaron was smiling without show-ing his teeth. "I knew Mom wouldn't go for it, so I told them not to tell her."

"You're lying!" I said, eyes squinting. "Why would anyone do that?"

"So I can join the circus when I'm sixteen and be in those freak shows."

"The ones on TV with the hairy fat ladies?" Danny asked.

"Yeah, those."

"You're full of shit," I said to Aaron.

"Look at my hand! Why do you think it's wrapped up so big?"

We both examined the bandage without touching it. Danny's head tilted like a puppy. Mom walked into the bedroom and swept us out. She whispered, "Let Aaron sleep," and then shut the door behind us. Danny and I looked at each other wide-eyed then sat down outside Aaron's bedroom door. We sat in silence, waiting for the bandage to come off his hand.

Manguera Wars

The rules were as always: no kick-
ing, scratching, biting, or pushing. Bobby's whistle started the round.
Wanting to impress my older brothers, I struck first. Danny got it in
the belly. He countered with a jab to my face. I hit his arm. Danny
punched my shoulder. I stumbled back and stepped on the orange
gravel that Aaron had taken from the neighbor's yard to mark off the
ring. Then I slid. One knee hit the rust colored spot where the gravel
had ground into the cement driveway. Danny charged toward me.

Bobby stepped between Danny and me. With a chopping gesture so familiar to me from the Lucha Libre bouts that my brothers
and I watched religiously on Sunday evenings, Bobby stopped the
fight and helped me up.

"Watch it man," Bobby pushed Danny. "Fight fair or I'll kick your
ass. Hear?"

Danny nodded.

Bobby whistled, and our match resumed. I boxed Danny's pointed ears. He socked my jaw. I poked his ribs and kept at them just like
Bobby coached.

"Go for the ribs," he shouted. "The ribs, Jenny!"

"Don't let her do that to you Danny," Aaron shouted. "What's
your problem?"

Danny kicked my pelvis, and both my brothers were on top of
him.

"What did we tell you, Spock?" Bobby straddled Danny, who lay
wriggling on the cement. He bent over, like a center taking a snap,
and pointed a finger at his eye.

"Don't call me that." Danny's voice quavered. He looked up at
our brothers and touched his ear. "I told you not to call me that. Let
me up, it burns."

"You gotta fight fair or else," Aaron said.

"Or else, what?" Danny wiped the sweat from his temples with his forearm and sat up. Bobby never moved, and when Danny sat up his eye hit Bobby's extended finger. "Ay, you asshole," Danny rubbed his eye with one hand and fanned his back with the other. "Why'd you poke my eye."

Bobby said, "I didn't poke it. You slammed into my finger." He placed a foot on Danny's thigh to keep him still.

"Screw this!" Danny batted the foot away and stood. When he tried to walk away, he was jerked to a stop by the green water hose tied around his waist. The other end was tied to my waist, and I was pulled forward and nearly fell.

Aaron screamed, "I see Mom's car!"

Danny and I frantically worked on the knots around our waists.

Bobby untied Danny and then me.

"Screw the manguera into the faucet," he yelled.

I grabbed the end of the hose and shoved it into the tap.

"No, stupid, the metal end," Bobby pointed.

"False alarm," Aaron sighed. "We can resume play."

"I don't wanna play," Danny and I said in unison.

"Why? You chicken, Jenny?" Aaron sneered.

The manguera snaked across the hard-packed dirt of our un-landscaped yard and across the glowing cement driveway. The drive was blinding to look at and impossible to step on. Bare feet burned on its surface.

"No, I'm just sick of boxing," I said. "And I'm hot."

"You're scared you might get your butt kicked," Aaron said.

I stood and heaved my chest out, just like I'd seen El Toro do last Sunday during his bout against El Rey, "I'll fight you right now without the manguera."

Bobby took one of my trembling arms, "Cool it, man. Mom will be home soon anyways."

Bobby walked away from us toward the street and eased him-self onto the curb, like you would in a tub filled with hot water. He was stuck at home with us ever since he had poured used anti-freeze into his radiator and it overheated. I followed him and sat down immediately. My butt burned through my jeans, but I didn't get up. Sweat beaded under my nose but still I sat. Danny stood next to us as Aaron kicked the rocks he had so carefully arranged for our ring.

"Stop it, will you?" Bobby said.

"What's with you?" Aaron whined, then stopped kicking the rocks.

Danny sat on the other side of Bobby, but popped up quickly.

"Hot, dummy," I snickered.

Instead of sitting, he crouched like the people in Mom's books about Vietnam. The sweat dripped down my face, into my eyes. I ran my finger over my head like a squeegee, then flicked the liquid off my fingers.

"Watch it," Bobby backhanded the air.

Danny ducked, lost his balance, and placed his hand on the cement to break his fall.

"Ay!" he yelped.

We all laughed.

"Hey, you remember the tackle football game we had yester-day?" Bobby asked no one.

"Ah, man, remember?" Aaron said, walking toward the curb. "I keep replaying Melón biting it in the tumbleweed."

"It had to be face first," Bobby hit his face with his hands. "His big head made it into the end zone though."

"No, man! The tumbleweed was out of bounds," Aaron flapped his arms wildly.

"It's good if it's on the line," Bobby said.

"I don't think so," Aaron said.

"NFL rules," Bobby added. "All regulation."

I leaned backward to catch Danny's eye. When he looked over at me, I put my finger to my lips to warn him not to correct Bobby.

Aaron was quiet. "Cheese, I got stickers all up and down my arms on that tackle," he said, pointing to his forearms, which had what looked like a rash.

"You? I picked his face for an hour and still didn't get half the 'pinos out," Bobby said, putting his finger on his face.

"He wasn't in school today," Aaron said.

"Poor fucker," Bobby said.

"Yeah," Aaron rubbed his forearm.

We watched a line of ants march under our legs. They were swarming to a pink piece of bubble gum, which was melting into thick cream on the asphalt. Bobby spit on the line of ants, and we all watched as the ants floated in the white foam.

"Aren't you bored, you guys?" Bobby said, watching the ants.

"I am," Aaron said, standing, swinging his arms. "I wish we had enough people to play baseball."

"We could play basket," Danny said.

"That wouldn't be fair. Me and Aaron would kill you two," Bobby pointed to us.

We agreed, never once thinking of dividing up the teams differently. We had it coming.

"Too bad," Bobby said, shaking his head.

We sat. After a few minutes of picking scabs, Bobby got an idea. "Let's find out who's the toughest."

"No, I don't want to," I said, dejected. "Look it my arms. Now look it yours and Aaron's and even Danny's? It won't be fair. You guys'll beat me."

"You don't even know what we're playing, Jenny. This isn't that kind of tough, anyways. It's more of a mental toughness. It's all about mind over matter." He touched his middle finger to his forehead. "You're smart. You can do this, too."

Everyone, including me, was intrigued.

"Okay, now," Bobby clapped his hands together. "Whoever can hold his hand on the street the longest is the toughest."

"What? There's no way I'm doing that," Danny said.

"Yeah, that's about what I expected from you," Bobby shook his head.

"I'll do it," Aaron said.

That's what I expected from Aaron. Ever since he had lost his finger, he tried hard to be the strongest, toughest, and best at everything. The first time he played football after the accident, he dislocated the finger of his left hand and snapped it back into place so he wouldn't stop the game.

All three of my brothers looked at me. I was the majority vote. If I said yes, then Danny would have to play. "Majority rule" as Bobby would say.

"There's really nothing physical about this," Bobby said, directing his attention to Aaron. "It's what you got right here that counts." He pounded his fist on his heart. "The trick is to think of other things and try to distract yourself. You remember the Kung Fu episode, where he had to lift the big pot . . ."

" . . . with the boiling liquid with his forearms." Aaron finished the sentence and flexed the muscles in his forearms. "It's my favor–ite."

"It would be," I said. "All right, Grasshopper, I'm in."

Aaron clapped, and Danny groaned.

"Here are the rules," Bobby pointed. "We'll play rock, scissors, paper to see who goes first."

Before thinking, I said, "No, if I'm gonna do this, we all go at the same time, and whoever's hand is on the street last wins." I added, "Is that okay?" I looked over at Bobby, who, to my relief, grinned and nodded.

We all prepared ourselves in different ways. Aaron slapped his hands together hard, trying to numb them; Danny blew on his hands; Bobby rolled his wrist in a circle to loosen his hand; and I sat still and placed my hands on my knees and stared at them.

"Ready?" Bobby asked.

We all nodded.

"Go!"

We all placed our hands squarely on the black asphalt. Danny whimpered like a dog and immediately took his hand off the street.

"You're out," I exhaled.

Aaron sucked air through his teeth. Bobby looked like he was grinding his teeth, and I sweated from my ears. Even before I had placed my hand on the street, I had felt its heat. Once on the ground, it stung like an entire ant colony was biting my palm, but I held firm.

Danny was jumping around excitedly and counting, "Fifty–eight, fifty–nine . . . "

To my surprise, Bobby lifted his hand off the street.

Aaron and I stared at one another, sweat dripped down my back and onto my jeans. Aaron grimaced so that he looked like he was going to the bathroom. My hand burned. I thought he was going to lift his hand, but then the grimace turned to a blank stare, and he looked slightly above me. He was looking directly at the sun. His eyes were watering, and I started to worry he would lose his eyesight. My palm ached, and I knew I would never be able to outlast Aaron. I lifted my hand. Aaron raised his just after mine.

"That was awesome," Danny shouted. "You almost beat Aaron."

"She really had you going, Aaron," Bobby said.

"I'll never lose to a girl," he hissed.

I tried to slap him, but he leaned back and I missed.

After fanning our hands and talking about the burn, we sat back down and watched ants. Then we watched cars go by.

Danny broke the silence, "We could play touch football."

"Ball's flat," I said.

"We could play soccer with the flat ball," Aaron offered.

"Soccer?" Bobby said. "Now there's a sport for fags." He bit a fingernail and spit it to the ground, then he stood up and started punching air.

"Watch my shadow," he said.

Aaron joined in, pumping his fists, and at times, their shadows connected. It looked like they were boxing. The two ducked, jumped, and head faked. Soon, Danny and I tried. We screamed every time our shadows met, and Bobby and Aaron crowded around us.

"I'll bet you can beat Danny up for real," Bobby said to me. "Because you're tall. Look at him, short people can't fight."

"Do you hear what Bobby's saying?" Aaron countered. "He thinks Jenny can beat you up. Are you gonna let a girl beat you up?"

Our shadowboxing got a little more intense. Danny got too close to my face, and his fist scraped my cheek. Mad, I pulled his hair, and he slapped at my hands.

"Cool it," Bobby said, sternly.

Aaron squeezed my hands so hard I had to let go of Danny's hair, which stopped our free-for-all.

"In order to settle this, you two need to fight," Bobby pointed with both hands. He dragged the manguera from where we had left it and tied the thin, faded green hose to my waist and knotted the other end to Danny's. "Rules are like always: no kicking, scratching, biting, or pushing."

"I think she wins, Aaron," Danny said, tapping his older brother on the elbow.

Aaron shoved Danny's hand off. "All right, all right then, you be the median. So, who we gonna contact?"

"Can we try Pooch?"

"No, stupid, it has to be a dead *person*," Jenny said.

"Then let's call Jesus," Aaron rubbed his chubby hands over his biceps.

"Ay, Aaron, he won't come because he's already here," said Jenny.

"He is? Where?" Aaron looked from side to side.

"Just shut up, will you? We got to contact someone scary and evil."

"What about . . . " Danny began.

"No, not the devil. We'll go to hell."

"Well, then how about Charles Manson?" Aaron pointed a finger in the air.

"He's not dead, dummy. They have to be dead."

"But he's scary, ¿qué no?" He ran his hands over the candle.

"Listen, if you guys aren't going to take it seriously, we're not going to do this."

"All right, all right, how about Chapo?"

After a few seconds of silence, Jenny said, "Why not? He's family. He won't hurt us."

"We don't know that. I heard he knifed a guy in La Tuna," Aaron said as he slashed Danny's side with the stub of his index finger.

Danny's eyes widened.

"That's a chance we'll have to take," Jenny sat straight.

"I don't want to take a chance," Danny said.

"I knew he wouldn't do it." Aaron poked Danny's chest. "We should have never included him."

"Shut up, Aaron. Listen, Danny, the spirits can't hurt us. They're just spirits, see, and all they do is talk."

"What do you wanna ask him?" Danny folded his arms.

"What?"

"What are we gonna ask? What do we need to know about from him?"

"We can ask him why he went to jail." Aaron karate chopped his little brother on the leg.

"Ay!" Danny pushed Aaron.

Aaron shoved Danny, and he tumbled to the center of the circle and knocked over the lit candle. It rolled on the linoleum floor. As it crossed the room, it seemed as if the flame painted above St. Jude's head grew, and then it ignited the shag rug underneath the tin TV tray.

Jenny grabbed a T-shirt from a laundry basket nearby and threw it on the flame. The fire ate the thin shirt and grew. Aaron fanned it, and it got bigger. Danny stumbled away from the fire toward the kitchen, as Aaron and Jenny grabbed family photos off the hot tin. Danny ran back into the room carrying an orange box, and dumping baking soda over the fire, he extinguished it. All three let out a sigh.

"Jenny?"

"Yeah?"

"I thought you said the spirits couldn't hurt us." Danny pushed his sister with the box of baking soda.

Man of the House

I was playing solitaire at the kitchen table when Mom stumbled inside, giggling. She had her arm wrapped around a man's thick waist.

"Oh, I thought you were at abuela's," Mom said, letting him go.

The dark, hairy man smoothed the hem of his wrinkled sports coat before he straightened himself up and walked over to me with an extended hand.

"Aurelio Longoria, good to meet you," he said.

His hairy knuckles tickled my palm. I wanted to jerk away, but I said, "Hi, I'm Nancy, and I was just leaving."

"No, you weren't, you were sitting here playing cards," he said, pulling out a chair.

This one wanted to impress my mother, I thought. So I held half a deck up in the air and said, "Wanna play?"

Mom squinted at me, and Aurelio clapped. "Chingado, I hope you two have lots of money because I could always use more," he said.

"You play poker?" Mom asked, grinning.

"That's like asking a borracho if he eats menudo." Aurelio turned the chair so that the spindles faced the table, straddled it, bounced on the seat, and then leaned his chest into its back.

Mom shrugged her shoulders and sat across from Aurelio at the kitchen table.

He did most of the talking, which was fine with me, because all I wanted to do was yell at Mom for missing a conference with my science teacher that we'd scheduled for that afternoon. I'd reminded her about the meeting before she'd left for work, then again when she'd picked me up for lunch. After an hour of playing, Aurelio stood and yawned.

"Mind if I stay?" He nodded at me.

I looked over at Mom, who smiled then stared at the floor. "I don't care," I lied.

"It's settled then," Mom said, as if she'd been holding her breath all night. "Get what you need for tomorrow from the bedroom, mija."

First, a no-show, and now this. I threw the deck of cards onto the table, spilling Mom's beer.

Aurelio leaned over Mom, embraced her, then said, "She's a teenager, amor. I know what they're like. Besides we've got this big room to ourselves." He picked her up off the floor and turned her around so that she faced the living room.

Mom reluctantly agreed.

I started to reach for his hand but then thought better of it. I cleaned up the spilled beer, instead. "I'll get you guys some blankets," I said, grateful that I wouldn't have Aurelio's smell on my sheets.

I slept soundly with my door locked. If Aurelio had any thoughts of midnight wandering, like some of the others, he'd have to break the door down, which would surely wake my mother.

The next morning, I was greeted by the scent of baloney and coffee. When I got to the living room, I saw Mom seated at the table. Aurelio saluted me from the kitchen.

"Good morning, amor." He had his pants on and mom's nylon half-slip. The waistband was just under his armpits, and black chest hair poked through the fabric. "You want some huevos?"

I laughed. "Sure, why not." I sat next to Mom, who just rolled her eyes.

"Where are your plates?" Aurelio said.

"I'll get them." I stood.

"No, no, amor." Aurelio opened and closed the cabinets. "Just sit there. Let the man of the house get you and your mom some breakfast."

Mom raised one eyebrow, and I smiled. He set the hot frying pan on top of the playing cards from last night. Aurelio spooned the egg, bean, and baloney mixture onto our plates. The grease spots on mom's slip made the fabric stick to his chest.

I asked, "What's this?"

"Smells good, no?" He smiled wide. "And it tastes better. It's the Aurelio especial."

"Ay, Aurelio, this reminds me of my honeymoon," Mom said, then hummed.

Trying to hide the curiosity in his voice, Aurelio asked, "When did you get married?"

"When I was very young and stupid." She stopped humming and sipped her coffee.

Aurelio sat. "Where did you get married?"

"Right in my mother's backyard. It was beautiful." Mom looked up at me from her coffee. "Your grandmother decorated everything in baby blue because that was my favorite color. I even made my own dress. Too bad the pictures aren't in color like they are now."

"Baby blue," Aurelio said. "That was the color of my tux at my second wedding. Segura you didn't marry me?"

Mom snickered, then turned from me to Aurelio. "Positive," she said. "It was the same week my oldest sister died . . . "

"Overdosed," I said.

Mom's face was tight, like a moño. "She didn't overdose, goddamn it, she froze to death. Her boyfriend brought her home all fucked up and just left her lying in the front yard, with no coat, shoes, nothing. It was during that freak snowstorm back in sixty-one. I found her the next morning. Tried to drag her inside by myself, but I was too small. I was too fucking small."

Aurelio reached across the table and squeezed her shoulder.

"I was fifteen, I think." Mom lifted her cup toward me. "As old as Nancy, and I couldn't get her inside."

Hoping to make Mom feel better, I said, "'She looked peaceful for the first time in her life,' was what abuela told me about it."

"How the hell would she know?" Mom set the cup on the table so hard coffee spilled out. "She wasn't there. She was never around. Carmen was blue and miserable. Who can be peaceful freezing to death?"

Aurelio massaged Mom's back in circles. I frowned.

Mom shrugged Aurelio's touches off.

"All this talk about la muerte," Aurelio said, as he dug into his eggs with his fork. "Reminds me of my brother. Ernie was only twenty-three, and he died in el bote. Rotted in jail, but we got to bury him here." He pointed to the floor. "In El Paso. At the funeral, my mom was crying buckets of tears. And my tío walks into the room. You know that one where only the family goes?"

I sighed and tried not to fidget.

"My tío just holds my mother, and she cries on him until she can't cry no more. Then he finally talks. He says, 'Death calls everyone, Colocha.' And all of us in the room nod, and he goes, 'That's why I don't have a phone.'"

Mom looked up, slapped his arm, and said, "Payaso. You're so silly."

I laughed out loud.

"N'ombre, we can't have everyone all sad, like this." Aurelio shook his head.

I piled a mouthful of eggs onto my spoon and ate, and for the first time in fifteen years, I was glad Mom had brought a man home with her.

Aurelio was still making breakfast for us a month later. Instead of using my mother's slip, he wore a green apron I'd bought him at a flea market that said "Man of the House." Every Sunday, after breakfast, we shopped. The Fox Plaza mercado had everything we needed. Mom bought groceries, I bought school clothes and supplies, and Aurelio talked to the old men, who sold used weed whackers, sinks, tires, and rusted chains. He had picked up the apron from the bed of a truck that had a pile of clothes and had shown it to my mother. She had taken it away from him, wadded it up, and thrown it back in the pile. "You're not working. What are you thinking?" she had said. Angry, I bought the apron as they walked ahead, and I gave it to Aurelio in the car on the ride home. Mom had looked at me out of the corner of her eye, but I didn't care. She was losing interest, and I couldn't do a thing to stop it. It was while we were eating breakfast, before one of our flea market trips, that Mom and Aurelio had their first fight.

"Come on, amor, it's only ten days." He pointed his knife at her.

"Ay, Aurelio, I can't leave Nancy that long."

"¿Qué chinga es eso? What does that mean? You leave her alone all the time. What's different? Nancy, you'll be all right if me and your mom go to Piedras?"

"Yeah," I said. "What's in Piedras?"

"That's where I'm from."

"Oh." I looked over at Mom and could tell by the way she had her eyes glued on her coffee cup that she wasn't interested in this trip.

Aurelio must have seen that vacant look in her face because he stopped eating and stared at her. Then he said, "It's not about Nancy."

"Don't talk to me that way."

"You don't like the truth?"

"You think I'm a bad mother and still you want me to meet your family? If you don't like the way we live, then leave," she said.

"Hey, hey, don't talk that way," he said.

Mom's olive complexion turned pink. "Go. You're starting to get on our nerves."

"You mean your nerves," he said. He started to get mad when Mom didn't answer. "What the fuck was I thinking? You and your gabacha ways. What am I doing? You're right."

He got up, grabbed a change of clothes out of the chest of drawers in my bedroom, and left. He stayed away for two days. Anytime Mom tried to talk to me during that time, I gave her short, curt answers, until she finally just left me alone. On the third day, when I woke up, Aurelio was in the kitchen frying eggs, and Mom was sitting at the table as if nothing had happened. So I sat too, afraid he was still mad.

"Wanna go out later? All three of us?" Aurelio asked.

I saw relief on my mother's face, too, and we both said, "Yeah."

"My cousin, Yvette, just moved, and she's having a party at her new place," Aurelio said, as he rubbed his hands together. "Vámonos. Let's all go play some poker then."

I could smell the cigarette smoke while we waited outside for Yvette to open the door. Aurelio whispered, "Don't mention nothing about Manny's eye."

Yvette opened the door and gave Aurelio a bear hug and then embraced my mother and me at the same time.

"Where you been? We've been waiting for you since two."

"We had to wait for la profesora over here—" Aurelio motioned toward me with his head—"to get out of school."

"Entren. Entren." Yvette pushed us inside.

When I walked into the cinderblock house, the haze of cigarette smoke made me cough, and I noticed that this place was no bigger than ours. The only furniture in the large living room was a lopsided tin table, with a red oval in the center that read "Corona" in black letters. Four gray Coca-Cola crates served as chairs. The house looked as bare as ours felt when I was home alone. Yvette didn't have any pictures or paintings to clutter up the white walls, and the single naked bulb that hung from the ceiling blinded anyone who looked up.

"Manny, this is Aurelio's novia, Marisol, and her daughter, Nancy."

"Mucho gusto," Mom and I said at the same time.

Manny, seated on a crate, waved to us with a deck of cards in his hand. Aurelio walked over to him and patted Manny on the back.

I sat on a piece of matted, orange shag carpet, while the others sat at the table. I had a view of the back of Aurelio's head and Manny's face. His fake eye stared straight at me. Mom sat to the right of Aurelio, and Yvette sat to his left. Manny dealt the cards as soon as they settled, and it seemed as if everyone talked at once. I was dizzy from the smoke, and the noise calmed me. The constant talk, laughter, and music made me feel invisible. I sat for two hours, softly singing with radio-station rancheras and untangling the fibers of the carpet.

"Mija, go get your tío Aurelio a cerveza." Mom's lids were heavy from too much beer. Her cheeks glowed like they did after she did sit-ups in our bedroom. The stupid look on her face didn't diminish her beauty. It added to it. Made her look like the sexy maids on TV who slept with their bosses.

I stood up and before going into the kitchen, I said, "If Aurelio is my tío, that would mean you're dating your brother."

Mom just laughed and continued to ignore me. So when I brought Aurelio's beer, I shook it a little and opened it behind her. It squirted her back.

"Pendeja!" Mom jumped out of her seat. "You did that on purpose."

"How was I supposed to know it was going to do that?"

"You shook it."

"No, I didn't."

There was silence in the room before Aurelio stood, took my mother by her slender arm, and kissed her cheek.

He turned to Manny, then said, "You see what I'm telling you, compa, I'm fucking charmed. I have this effect on women. They fight over me."

"Yeah, they fight to get away from you," Yvette said, and everyone laughed, even Mom.

"I think we all need some beer, Nancy," Aurelio said, touching my head.

After I brought everyone beer, I settled back into my corner, thinking about how I was going to scratch all my mother's favorite albums.

"You know, carnal, I fell off the roof trying to fix the fucking aire," Aurelio explained, as he swayed from side to side. "Fell down the motherfucker like a bowling ball y me di un golpe right on my knee. It hurt like hell." He clutched his knee.

Manny grinned so that I couldn't tell if he was happy or mad. I didn't think it was a good idea for Aurelio to go up on our roof to fix the swamp cooler, but Mom insisted since he was home all the time.

"It got all swollen and shit." Aurelio hiked up his green Dickies and set his leg on the table. "My knee was the size of a melón. I had to call in sick."

The tin table buckled toward the center from the weight of his leg. All the pennies and two ashtrays slid into the depression and got mixed up.

"Look what you did," Manny said, his meaty finger pointed to the pennies on the table.

"Ay, Aurelio, get your pierna off the table already. No one wants to see your hairy leg." Mom pinched him.

Weary of Manny and his eye, I scooted so that I was behind Mom.

With his leg still on the table, Aurelio continued, "The next day I went to work. It was killing me. There was no way I would be able to drive the truck. Then it hit me," he said, slapping his head with his hand, "man, I can get some feria out of this shit. I lifted myself into my truck and then, I just let go. I let myself fall. I fell right on my knee. It hurt like a son of bitch. I had fucking tears in my eyes."

Manny shuffled the deck of cards. Yvette's pencil thin brows furrowed in concern between puffs of a cigarette.

"Then all the guys gathered around me and helped me up. I went up to the jefe, Stan, a big gabacho, and told him what happened. He whipped out the workman comp papers and made a phone call. My carnal drove me to the clínica, and the doctor told me I would be out for at least four weeks. Now, I'm on easy street, man." Aurelio added, with four raised fingers, "Four weeks of paid vacation."

Yvette and Mom clapped and cheered, but Manny just nodded.

I didn't think Aurelio's story was funny either, knowing how Mom would pick me up from school some days, and we'd drive around for hours just to get some peace and quiet before heading home.

"Ay, Aurelio, that's enough talk. We need to get home." Mom shifted in her seat uncomfortably.

A few hours later, they all looked tired. Yvette and Mom had stopped smiling, and Manny and Aurelio droned on and on about some war.

"Where the hell were you when I was off fighting for your freedom, pendejo!" Manny's face was red as he pointed a stubby finger toward Aurelio.

"I think I was getting laid." Aurelio touched his groin.

"Yeah, everything is a joke to you, isn't it?" Manny opened his arms and looked as if he were going to hug the entire table. "While you were off probably faking injuries and shit, I was fighting for your freedom. Fighting for the white government that you, and the rest of the lazy asses like you, are so quick to criticize. I lost my best friend in that fucking war."

Bored, Mom turned to me and said, "We're leaving in a little while. Why don't you go lie down? You look sick."

She had no idea how sick I was. Sick of taking care of things, of being ignored, of being taken for granted, of being used, and mostly, of her. Hurting, I lay down like she said.

"Yeah," Aurelio said. "It was probably Yvette's tamales. She uses Smith's meat in them, and you never know what you're getting from the gabacho butcher."

"I'd rather go there than to that marijuano Cárdenas," Yvette said.

"There he goes again with that gabacho shit. It's all a big fuck-ing conspiracy. Yeah, man, Whitie is out to get you. I'm half white, ése." Manny pointed to himself. "I bet you didn't know that."

"Oh, yeah," Aurelio said, putting his cards on the table. "Which half?"

"A big fucking joke—that's what life is to Aurelio. We're all one big fucking joke," Manny threw his cards on the table in disgust. "Even my wife's food, he makes fun of."

"Compa, all I'm saying is that you'd still have your eye and your friend if you didn't get yourself mixed up in their pinche war."

Manny stood and kicked the crate behind him so hard it slammed into the wall, then he calmly turned to Yvette and said, "It's time for your cousin to leave."

It was the calm that scared me. I remembered Mom's boyfriend, the one before Aurelio; he would get calm, talk in a low voice like Manny did, just before he'd take a swing at one of us. We'd have to run either outside or into our bedroom. He never followed us through the door, but we'd stay there until he left. I touched Mom's elbow, and she gave me her hand to hold.

"Come on, compa," Aurelio pleaded. "We're all drunk."

"I'm not your compa. Get the fuck out of my house, and take those bitches with you."

Mom lifted me, and we both stood. As we walked out the door, she said, "Thanks for inviting us, Yvette."

We left Aurelio inside with his cousin and Manny. I kept my mouth shut as we got in the car. A few seconds later Aurelio came out of the house.

On the drive home, he said, "You believe that Manny? That house isn't his. Yvette put the down payment."

Mom looked back at me and rolled her eyes.

I gave her a dirty look before I gripped the backseat next to Aurelio's ear so hard my knuckles went numb.

"Why can't you shut up?" I said. "Just shut up for once. You'd be a half way decent guy if you'd just shut the fuck up. You ever wonder why you don't have a wife? It's because people get sick of you, you and your mouth. You talk so much they don't want to be around you."

"I don't have a wife because, because I don't want a wife." He tried to look at me in the backseat, but the car swerved, and he looked forward again. "It's not me that can't get dates. Why don't you have a boyfriend? You ever asked yourself that question?"

"Why would I want a boyfriend? So I can watch him act like an asshole when he gets drunk with his friends?"

"Your mother's not always going to be here, you know."

"Aurelio, just who the fuck do you think you are talking to my daughter that way?"

"Now you speak up? You're taking her side? I see the way it is. I'm a fucking pendejo for not seeing it before, but I get it."

"Well, at least we agree on something." I rolled down the window.

"You won't have to worry about this asshole much longer. I'll leave. I'll leave tonight."

"Why don't you?" Mom turned to me and winked.

—————————

The next day, as I was getting ready for school, Mom poked her head in the bathroom. Her large eyes narrowed.

"I don't understand why you work so hard, mija," she said.

I didn't answer. As I rubbed the thin white towel on my moist skin, I watched her face.

She inhaled deep and blew the breath out of her nose. It made a whistling sound.

"You know, I feel kind of sick today."

"You do?" She touched my forehead. "Maybe you should stay home?"

I nodded.

"I'll write you a note for tomorrow. And maybe we can listen to Freddy."

Freddy Fender was Mom's cure for aches—stomach, head, or heart. I crawled into my bed with her, she wrapped her arms around me, and we listened to "When the Next Teardrop Falls."

"Do you like school?"

"No."

"Neither did I."

We listened to the familiar nasal voice singing, "I'll be there any time you need me. . . ." Mom squeezed me tight.

"What are you going to write on my note?" I kicked my legs.

"That you had the stomach flu."

"You wrote that last time." I raised myself up. "You can't write that again."

"Ay, mija, they don't care. They just want a note."

"Yes, they do. They save them all in your file. It's a file that follows you through life, even up to college. What if I wanna go someday?"

"You worry too much, mija. You remind me of abuela. Always on my ass."

I got up to change the record. I tried to pull Anne Murray's Greatest Hits from its album cover, but the record got hung up on the paper sleeve, so I ripped it. I wanted to tell Mom that she needed to be more like abuela. That I was sick of reminding her what to write on my notes for school. That I was tired of telling her to pay the bills. That she was spending too much money. That Aurelio was right—she doesn't like the truth.

When I finally got the record out of its sleeve, Mom asked, "What's wrong? I'm here. You can tell me anything."

I shook my head.

Mom woke me up at midnight. Wanted me to take a ride with her. I stumbled putting on my sweat suit, while she giggled watching me. I hopped around more than necessary to keep her spirits up. She hadn't brought anyone home since Aurelio left, and I was worried about her. She stopped at Peter's store on the corner to buy a carton of eggs. Then we drove in her car.

"That son of a bitch thinks I'm stupid." Mom gripped the steering wheel. "Thinks I don't know where the hell he's been this past week. Do you think I'm stupid, mija?"

"No, no way, Mom. You're the smartest person I know."

"That's right, honey. And to think this asshole—asshole!—thinks he can fuck me and then turn around and fuck that woman. She's not even a woman; she's a cow. You should see her. She must weigh at least one ninety. Look at me. Look at me Nancy. Am I a cow? Well, am I?"

"No, you're not. You're beautiful, Mom. You remind me of a movie star." I thought of Marilyn Monroe, Rita Hayworth, and Joan Crawford, and I wondered if all beautiful women were cursed.

"Ay, mija, you're sweet. The reason I look this way is because I take care of myself, and if you take care of yourself, too, you could look just like me." She turned to me and caressed a lock of my hair. "When we get home we're going to do something with that hair, okay? I promise."

"Okay."

I helped her search for Aurelio's car in the driveways of the houses we passed. I wanted to see for myself if the son of a bitch was cheating on my mother.

"¿Te gustan las morenas gordas, motherfucker?" Mom said to the night air.

"There it is." I pointed to a silver car in a driveway.

"No, that's a Continental."

As we drove, I looked at myself in the vanity mirror. I must have my father's face, I thought. Mom was a beautiful woman, and she could be with anyone. But always, in the end, she had nobody. All Aurelio had wanted was for her to meet his family. How bad could that be?

The car came to a complete stop, and I hit my face on the mirror then slid off the seat. His Buick was parked on the lawn of a
brick house. I got out of the car with the carton of eggs and started
to pitch. After hitting his car with the last egg, I ran back to Mom's
car, opened the door, and crawled inside.

Breathing hard, I said, "Who needs him? Hairy-knuckled motherfucker can go fuck a cat for all I care."

A Scenic Night

Legs up on the dashboard, bare feet making toe prints on the windshield inside a banana–yellow Chevette, Sandra and Yvette giggled, making the car bob up and down. Whenever Sandra got in a fight with Chano about his visiting their three–year–old daughter, Alma, the girls took a trip up to Scenic Drive. They drove up the mountain at least once a week. At night, the view from atop the Franklins always lifted their spirits. They saw where the yellow lights of El Paso stopped and the high glow of the white lights of Juárez began. A perfect line running east and west that divided the two cities and people. In the daytime, the line disappeared, and both cities looked like one looming industrial plant.

"No, seriously, Sandra, if you want to stop the nosebleeds, you have to shove your middle finger up your nose as far as it'll go." Yvette flipped the bird at Sandra, with her chorizo–sized finger.

"Does it have to be Vaseline? Can't you just use crema," Sandra said. "Vaseline is so thick."

"That's the point, it'll coat your nostrils," Yvette slapped her hands on her fat thighs. "If you want your wedding dress ruined when you get a nosebleed, then do it your way. You'll have to pay chingos of money to the photographer to touch up the pictures."

"Whenever I get married, I'm wearing black anyway, so it don't matter," Sandra said.

"You'll pass out from dehydration before you even make it to the altar." Yvette tapped her foot on the glass in front of her. "You know, I read where some scientists from Cambridge did a study on heat and what it does to the body."

"You read?" Sandra tapped back.

"You're so funny." Yvette's foot tapped faster on the glass. "They found out that the heat can make people crazy."

"Does it even get hot up there?" Sandra's bare feet were still.

"Where?" Yvette said. "What are you talking about?"

"In Cambridge." Sandra squeezed her toes into the window until they were white. "It's in Connecticut or somewhere, right?"

"That's not what matters." Yvette put her legs down. "What the point is, is that they found out that the heat makes people nuts and they can't think straight."

"I believe that. I've seen you around guys and you can't talk, let alone think."

Yvette said, "Ay, it's no use trying to be smart. You're just too dumb. Change the subject."

Sandra lifted an eyebrow. "Remember when I'd give you free drinks at the bar."

Yvette sat up in the car seat. "Yeah, those were good times."

"I knew it was time to split when the drunks I served started asking me for money to buy beer," Sandra laughed.

"How old were you?" Yvette said, poking the glass in front of her with her big toe.

"I was fifteen. Remember, I lied and told them I was nineteen." Sandra jabbed her foot in the air. "That fucker . . . "

Yvette interrupted, "Who? Chano?"

"No, stop. I don't want to think about him." Sandra sighed. "Steve, Steve, my manager, Steve. He told me I wasn't pretty enough to be hostess. I'd make a better waitress because even though I wasn't too pretty, I wasn't so bad that men didn't want me around."

"And you stayed?" Yvette asked, incredulous. "Why didn't you ever tell me that?"

Sandra shrugged.

Yvette snorted out loud. "I remember your first day. That fat fucker," Yvette sucked air into her mouth so that her cheeks were round, then said in a low voice, "'Sandy, you're going to have to raise that hem line.' The look on your face!"

"I'm so glad you were there. No one would have believed me." Sandra moved the knob on the broken radio.

"I would've." Yvette took Sandra's hand. "Men are capable of anything," Yvette said.

Sandra sang in a falsetto, "But it's above my knees." And she pointed to her legs.

Yvette boomed, "We're trying to sell liquor here, we're not playing ball!"

Both girls laughed and stamped their feet on the windshield. They stopped when they heard a crack. After inspecting the glass for damage, they giggled some more.

"You would have looked so good if you would have just let me hem the shorts up to your butt like I wanted," Yvette said, with her hands in a prayer position.

Sandra slapped her best friend's hands, not wanting to read the green letters below her knuckles. "Yeah, it was when I was pregnant with Alma." Sandra pointed to her seat. "But I didn't want my ass all hanging out while I was working. I wouldn't have been able to serve shit thinking about it. I still have the scar from where you poked me with the needle. Sí tú, Miss Seamstress."

The girls slapped at each other then stopped.

When their panting was the only sound in the car, Yvette spoke up. "Why don't we go out?" She pointed toward Mexico.

"We are out." Sandra raised her hands in the air so that her palms faced the windshield. She dropped her hands. "*He'll* be there, and I got to get back and put Alma to bed."

Yvette whispered, "You know your mom's already got her down. It's Friday, no school tomorrow. Come on, let's just go. We'll go all spontaneous."

Sandra shook her head, then she gripped the steering wheel and looked straight ahead. "All right then, vámonos."

———————

Inside the adobe room, was a blitzkrieg of lights, drinks, chatter, and dancing. The girls had to scream into each other's ears to talk. They sat at the plywood bar, and the bartender poured them drinks without asking what they wanted.

"Red light, green light," he said, then passed the girls a red and a green drink, and he took a yellow one for himself.

Sandra kept one eye on the door, waiting for Chano, and the other on the dance floor. A man asked Yvette to dance. The minute she stepped onto the dance floor, Yvette nuzzled her pelvis into the man's crotch. He held her waist. Sandra watched Yvette tease the man, who looked like he was about to pass out from all the grinding.

"Your friend likes viejos?" the bartender yelled in Sandra's ear.

"Yeah, I guess we both do," Sandra yelled back.

"Is twenty–five old enough?" The bartender pointed to him–self.

"Not old enough," Sandra screamed and looked at the doorway to see who was arriving. She saw Chano walk through the door with a young girl. Sandra spilled her drink. The bartender handed her his white towel.

He leaned over the bar and said, "You know him?"

Sandra nodded and watched Chano pull out a chair for the teenager, who was several years younger than Sandra. He looked up and caught Sandra's eye, then grinned.

She smiled and turned back to the bartender, who used his index finger to tell her to come closer. When Sandra leaned into the bar, he kissed her. She was grateful, sad, and excited. When she opened her eyes after the kiss, Chano was standing next to her. Not looking her way, he just tried to order at the bar.

The bartender slapped his towel down, "You'll have to wait; I'm taking a break." The bartender walked around the bar and took Sandra's hand, then led her toward the door.

Outside Sandra felt nauseated. She stopped and crouched near a truck to put her head down, waiting for the sick feeling to leave. The bartender opened the truck door, lifted Sandra and set her on the seat, then he got in with her. Inside, he pulled her pants down to her knees. Sandra did not resist. She did not move. She did not make a sound. He groped at his pants, found what he was looking for, and then came before he entered her.

Sandra laughed. "You really are a viejo."

"Shut up, bitch," the bartender said pulling up his pants. "That's the last time I do anybody any favors."

"Hey, I didn't mean anything. I'm just playing around. Don't leave."

He opened the truck door, got out, then slammed it shut. It felt like a slap on Sandra's face. She sighed, used a dirty pair of socks on the floorboard to wipe herself off and then pulled up her pants. When she got out of the truck, she saw Yvette scanning the parking lot. Sandra waved.

"Where you been, bitch?" Yvette said. "When I saw Chano, I thought you left me."

"Don't call me that!" Sandra said. "I'd never leave you."

"Huh," Yvette said. "Let's go home, yeah?

The two girls walked side-by-side. They passed a liquor store and a taco stand, and stepped over men lying on the sidewalk, who smelled like lime and vomit. Nearly at the tollbooth to cross back into El Paso, Yvette tripped. Sandra caught hold of Yvette's tattooed hand to keep her from falling. She grabbed the tips of Yvette's brown, stubby fingers and squeezed them together. The rings on her own hand scratched, and Sandra wanted to let go, but she kept her grip.

Sandra was there when Yvette got the tattoo on her fingers. She wanted to tell her to stop, but Yvette was so angry, drunk, intent. She watched as Yvette's step-dad defiled and scarred her best friend. The hands that were Sandra's comfort during thirty-six hours of labor were no longer the same. Now, whenever Yvette made a fist, her right hand read F-U-C-K and the left read T-H-E-M. These were the same hands that had touched, poked, prodded, slapped, or caressed Sandra every day of her life since the second grade, except for the two weeks in junior high when Yvette had the chicken pox.

Yvette stayed upright then giggled—her breath a puff of smoke.

Sandra turned her head to look into her friend's hazel eyes— eyes that were lined with her charcoal-colored eyeliner on the inside of the eyelids, and on the outside corners, like Cleopatra.

"These fucking sidewalks, man," Yvette said, the tip of her purple fingernail pointing to the uneven cement.

Sandra nodded her head north, "Yeah, you'd think they'd know how to pave sidewalks, as many of them that work over there."

After a few steps, Sandra let go of Yvette's hand. "That bartender came all over me."

"So that's where you were," Yvette said. "I was wondering."

"I didn't really want to," Sandra said.

"Why'd you go?" Yvette asked. "Nevermind. Stupid question."

"I couldn't stop," Sandra said.

"You really love him?" Yvette said.

Sandra closed her eyes, and tears streamed down from the corners.

"Ay, Sandra you got to stop." Yvette made a fist with one hand. "My step–dad told me this after my mom left him, 'You know, chula, some people watch life pass them by y otros, they take life by the balls and squeeze every last seed out of it.' Of course, the motherfucker was leading my hand toward his balls as he was saying it, but I never forgot the meaning."

"I know. I know," Sandra snorted and wiped her eyes. "So which kind are you?"

Yvette showed Sandra the palm of her hands, which were callused and dry from her work at the hotel, scrubbing floors and toilets. "How do you think my hands got this way?"

Their laughter filled the night air. The two girls looked drunk.

"You got a dime?" Yvette pointed to the tollbooth.

"No, just a quarter." Sandra stepped toward the turnstiles and set the quarter on the counter. "I got to go on with my life." A dark hand with grime under the fingernails shot out from underneath the clear plastic window, covered the quarter, then slid it inside.

"How old you think that girl was?" Yvette ran her nails up Sandra's thin arm.

Sandra shrugged.

"She did look kind of young, no?" Yvette said.

Sandra had goose bumps as she said, "Nooooh! How old was the grandpa you were dancing with?"

"Maybe thirty–five," Yvette said.

"Válgame, Yvette that's almost as old as—" Sandra broke off.

She frowned at the man in the tollbooth who was picking a nickel out of a steel box. He put his fat lips on the coin, then stepped outside. Sandra waited for her change. Holding the nickel between his thumb and index finger, the man pressed the coin into Sandra's palm and said, "Wanna come home with me?"

Sandra snapped her hand shut then walked past him.

"How about you?" he looked at Yvette.

Yvette moved the turnstiles with her hips and said, "You wish, viejo!"

He clucked his tongue, which made Sandra cringe and grind her teeth. Every man she had ever met or dated could whistle, cluck, and suck air through his lips louder than the cars they drove with no mufflers, she thought. Yvette's long nails tickled Sandra's back, and she sped up.

"Why do men do that?" Sandra sighed.

"Because they're assholes." Yvette turned back to see the man looking at them. "Plain and simple."

Sandra closed her eyes in disgust. "She must have been thirteen."

"No, I don't think the girl even started, yet," Yvette added.

"It might as well have been Alma."

"Don't say that!" Yvette shook her head. "Don't ever say that about your own daughter. Chano's a mamón but he'd never."

"All those fucking Juarenses like 'em young," Sandra said, waving her hand in the air.

Three boys surrounded the girls as they left the turnstiles.

"You got any change?" a boy with a harelip asked.

Sandra said, "What?"

"Hey, baby, got a quarter?" an eight-year-old boy said as he pulled on the hem of Sandra's shirt. "Come on, Miss, give me some money. I'm hungry. I haven't eaten all night."

An older teenage boy, about Sandra's age, stood next to the eight-year-old but didn't say a word.

Yvette waded through the rail-thin boys and kept walking. "I hate those dirty—"

"You little shit get away—from—me!" Sandra yelled.

She held the forearm of the eight-year-old behind her, while the older teenager tried to put his hands inside the front pockets of her jeans. Sandra kicked at the teenager as the boy with the harelip cupped her breast. Sandra let go of the eight-year-old, who immediately tried to put his hand back into her pocket. She balled her hands as much as her long nails would allow and shot her fists in front of her, hitting chests, the top of heads, arms, whatever she found. The boys kicked and punched back. The boy with the harelip had a bloody forehead, cut from one of Sandra's rings. Yvette stepped into the scuffle, grabbed the eight-year-old, and pushed him to the ground. The boy with the harelip tried to get his hands in her pockets, and she slapped him away. The older boy grabbed hold of Yvette's long hair so that she was bowing to get out of his grip. After slapping at him several times, he released her hair. She grabbed one of Sandra's flailing arms and pulled her forward. Sandra stumbled a bit, regained her footing, and like Yvette started to run up the urine-stained sidewalk of the Santa Fe Bridge toward El Paso. The boys did not follow but yelled, "¡Putas!"

Sandra and Yvette did not stop running until they made it to the middle of the bridge. Winded, Yvette sat on the concrete marker that showed the boundary between Texas and Mexico. Sandra leaned her backside against a chain-link fence and breathed hard.

"You look like you're smoking," Yvette panted.

"I could use a cigarette about now," Sandra said, rubbing her hands together. "I'm cold."

"Me, too," Yvette looked up at Sandra.

"You'd be warm right now if you had let me bring my jacket, stupid!" Sandra frowned thinking about her windbreaker lying over Alma's crib. The red lipstick Yvette wore, the same color as on Sandra's lips, was smeared across the right side of Yvette's face. Sandra chuckled.

"That ratty jacket don't keep anything warm," Yvette tossed her hand in the air. "Besides who needs a jacket when we're just going for a cruise? You probably would have left it somewhere, and right now you'd be dragging my ass back to the other side, and we'd never get home."

"No, those little shits back there would have stolen it!" Sandra pointed south.

Yvette laughed. "Yeah, probably."

"I told them to shut the fuck up and leave me alone," Sandra said.

Yvette put her hands on her hips. "No wonder. Why'd you say that?"

"I don't know," Sandra waved her hand over her head. "I just got sick of 'em, you know?"

"I know." Yvette sat in silence.

The fight near the turnstiles had reminded Sandra of circus

clowns. Arms flying everywhere but missing all the other clowns. She always felt that way. Like she could never connect with someone. She had remembered one of those silly painted-faced men coming right up to her and giving her a balloon. It was one of the first things she could ever remember having gotten from a man. It wasn't one of those round balloons but one shaped like a dog, a little curly-haired dog, like rich ladies own. She still had the dog. It was just a long balloon, not any shape now, but she had it tucked away in her Bible under her bed. The balloon and Alma were all men were good for, she thought. Yvette's smeared face struck Sandra as funny, and she laughed. A blast of white smoke shot out of Sandra's mouth, and this made Yvette smile and rub her hands together for warmth.

They both laughed, and they both dabbed underneath their eyes with their middle fingers upwards and out. Yvette made fists and put them together in front of Sandra's face. Sandra looked down, not wanting to see, but mouthed "Fuck them." Sandra and Yvette continued to walk down the bridge and leaned into one another for support.

"Why is it so cold at night?" Yvette rubbed her arms together.

"I read somewhere that these Alaskans did a study and found out that it gets cold here at night so that all the people who have gone crazy in the daytime will say, 'El Paso's not so hot,' and stay."

"You read?" Yvette slapped Sandra's arm.

Enough

Lithium was the drug that tía Manuela took when she lived in Big Spring for six months. Doctors said it would curb her craving for beer and ease her paranoia. She stopped drinking beer all right—switched to vodka and drank a fifth a day. Mom didn't mind her drinking in the house because it kept her from wandering the streets. It was the spells she couldn't stand. Nothing could bring Manuela out of her spells. Mom said our place sounded like a nuthouse whenever Manuela hugged her legs to her chest and sat humming, rocking back and forth for hours. Once Mom got so fed up with it she grabbed hold of Manuela's arm and dragged her off the couch. Manuela hit her head on the coffee table and bled all over the carpet but continued to hum and rock. After that Mom left Manuela alone when she went into herself. When she sat next to me during one of her spells, I would rub her back. She seemed to like it, but I liked it more.

"Lo está haciendo adrede," Mom said, flashing me an accusing look.

I stopped rubbing her back, stretched my T-shirt over my bare legs, and watched TV. I wished Mom was the crazy one, just so that she would stick around and I could rub her back.

"Something's got to be wrong with a baby that was born in a toilet." Mom flipped her hands in the air, and her silver bracelets clinked as she looked at Manuela. "I should have let her flush your sorry ass."

My grandmother, Chela, long since dead, gave birth to Manuela while sitting on the commode. I got this kind of information out of Mom in bits and pieces throughout my life. It's how I got most of my family history.

When Manuela ran out of vodka or money, she would hit the streets. She'd be lost for days. Sometimes we'd see her at an intersection, and when she'd wander up to our car and tap on the window, Mom would make me lock my door. Manuela's black hair was dusty gray from sleeping outside. Her skin was a dark red, weathered from the heat and wind. I looked over her head toward the shiny strip mall we never shopped in, but it was hard to ignore my tía like Mom wanted me to do, with that familiar toothless grin just inches away from my face. I waved, hoping she would recognize me, but she just laughed. It sounded like a hen's clucking. Her brown lips curved into her mouth where her front teeth used to be. She had lost them in a fight. I was just another person refusing to give her money, so she walked away to the car behind us. Instead of crying, I thought about the bad things Manuela said to me. Like when we were collecting lizard tails, and I asked her who my father was.

"Who the fuck knows, Gorda?" She breathed heavy and clicked her tongue as she crouched to catch the lizard in front of her. She missed. "Shit."

"Got one!" I said after I stomped my foot on the spotted lizard, and it scurried away, leaving the writhing tail behind like a discarded jacket.

"Aha!" she laughed. "You know who met him?"

I was still.

"Chela."

"Chela? Abuela Chela?"

Manuela nodded. "I think they even ate at the house before your mom and him got married. But she didn't like that he sold drugas." She crouched low. "These fuckers are getting harder to catch."

I wanted to ask her if it was Mom or abuela who didn't like the idea of my father selling drugs, but all I said was, "It's almost winter."

"I ought to charge the bruja double for these." She pointed to the three lizard tails draped over her forefinger.

As if the curandera heard her, a dust devil cropped up. The mini-tornado traveled fast, and Manuela and I both looked at one another before we ran after it. She was faster and jumped right in the middle of the dusty whirlwind where she danced until the funnel-shaped dust storm played itself out. Her lime-green polyester pants shined in the sun and her pink T-shirt flapped in the wind, exposing her round, lumpy belly. She fought the wind in a Marilyn-Monroe stance.

"You see, she heard you," I said too loud.

"¡Mierda! It's a bunch of hocus-pocus crap."

Manuela didn't believe in the healing powers of Tijerina. She collected lizard tails for the curandera in exchange for a bottle of vodka, and she did this when she was low on cash.

"Yeah, well, how do you explain Mom getting better after getting a massage from her?"

"Any chiropractor could have done that. Your mom said so herself." Manuela clicked her tongue and pointed at me, "She just didn't have seventy-five bucks."

"Right, but how do you explain her finding twenty dollars at the store after the massage?"

"Luck."

"Exactly. Luck made from the curandera."

"Well, if you're such a believer, why don't you go ask Tijerina where the hell your father is?"

"Maybe I will."

"You won't."

I didn't have a father as far as Mom was concerned. She never told me who he was, and I never asked. Not because I didn't want to know, because, believe me, I did. I wanted to know where I got my dried-out hair, my Indian nose, and long middle toe because it sure wasn't from Mom. Mom looked like a Mexican Jane Russell. I never asked because anytime I tried to bring up the subject, Mom would get upset and split. She always came back a few days later, but it would scare me so bad, I'd clean up and make dinner for a week without being told.

The times Mom left, I wandered with Manuela. We would take the Sun Metro from the strip mall close to the house down south to Alameda. The bus dropped us off across the street from Manuela's favorite bar. Whenever I saw the bar's neon sign with the name "Carmen," my mouth watered because I knew I would be drinking a Coke with two cherries. The blonde lady outlined in neon held her wide skirt up and kicked her leg high whenever the sign was lit. Sometimes Carmen, the bar owner, didn't have the money to replace a burned out section of neon, and the blonde looked like she had only one leg.

"¿Quieres una coca?" Manuela asked before we walked into the dark bar. When we were on the south side, she only spoke Spanish. Manuela drank Tequila Sunrises made with vodka, and waited for hours until one of the red-nosed men slid next to her. I walked over to play with Angelina, one of the ten kids who lived in the white cinderblock house next door. We played in the empty sandlot on the other side of the bar. The green, prickly tumbleweeds that grew wild were aliens from outer space that wanted to experiment on us or impregnate us.

When I walked back from next door, a man in white overalls with paint stains was sitting next to my tía. I sat in the booth across from them and watched as they sang along with Vicente. The guy was actually good. I saw tears in his eyes when he cried out, "volver, volver, volver. . . ." After his performance, he wanted to go for a ride. Manuela nodded her head at me, and I followed. As I jumped into the back of his truck, he said the drinks at the bar were too expensive. We stopped at Western Beverage for a case of beer and some vodka. He didn't buy me anything, and then he drove us to the levy.

He backed his truck as close to the río as possible without plunging into the water. They sat on the bed of his Ford, and I was on the roof. The noon sun heated the metal so that it burned through my cutoffs. Both doors were open and his stereo blared Radio Mexicana loud enough for the people on either side of us to enjoy. They kissed and laughed, and I watched four kids about my age from the other side of the río swimming in the muddy water. I handed Manuela the vodka from the brown paper sack next to me when she needed a refill, and I handed him a warm beer whenever he asked for another. Thirsty, I drank half of Manuela's fifth, straight from the bottle. I got a headache shortly after, and the last thing I remember was hitting my head against the hard dirt.

Mom laughed when Manuela brought me home drunk. My tía

held me until I couldn't throw up anymore, and then put me to bed. I was afraid Mom would be gone when I woke up, so I tried to stay awake, but before I knew it, I was dead asleep.

Mom was in the kitchen fixing a drink when I woke up the next afternoon. My head hurt and my tongue was so dry it felt furry.

"Your tía's gone again. Where'd you two go yesterday?"

"Carmen's."

She lifted her freshly plucked brows and smiled. "I met someone, too. He's picking me up in a few minutes."

I bit my lip to keep from crying, and she stopped talking.

"Thirsty?" She passed her drink under my nose.

I retched up nothing over the kitchen sink. She laughed, then walked away to finish packing. I washed out her Coke can and filled it with water.

"You two drink too much water!" Mom yelled from the bedroom.

Mom never drank water. She passed out at the store once. The doctor told her she was dehydrated; she needed to drink more water and lay off the Cokes. She had ignored the doctor, and I ignored her and went into the living room to play with my Barbies.

I stacked Mom's double live albums into a square; then I stuck some of her Stayfree maxi pads to the walls of the makeshift room. My Western Barbie had her very own rubber room, like Manuela. I'd stick her in there whenever she had a nervous breakdown. She had lots of them because Anita, the Pac–N–Sav Barbie whose legs didn't bend, could get Ken's rocks off. He was always sneaking off to see her behind Barbie's back. I cut off Anita's beautiful long brassy hair during one of my beautician days. I made Ken like Anita's mohawk. It made her dangerous. Ken also liked the fact that Anita wanted sex all the time. She and Ken would go to porno theaters that I made from old Ohio Players albums, like "Honey" and "Fire." Mom's narrow foot in her stiletto heels kicked over the double albums.

"What the hell do you think you're doing?" Mom put her hands on her hips. The seven silver bracelets she wore on each wrist jangled. She was nervous and in a hurry. It was the first date she had had with an educated man. Her college class was finally beginning to pay off. When I didn't answer, she looked at her plastic black watch before she put out her thin hand. I gave her the doll. She held my Barbie by her matted platinum hair and walked away. I imagined my Barbie was in pain. As an afterthought, Mom walked back to me, bent down, and picked up my Coke can with her free hand. I used it to drink *that* water.

"You're not normal, mija." It came out sounding resentful, sad, and hurt, all at the same time.

As far as Mom was concerned, I was one cup of water away from the nuthouse. She insisted the tap water was to blame for making tía Manuela and me nuts. El Paso water was legendary. It was so hard it could rub the baby hairs off your face if you let it hit you right from the spout.

As if she could see my thoughts, she said, "If they can pour lithium in the water without asking us, who knows what the hell else they put in there." Mom looked at the Coke can in her hand. "And that profesor of mine is full of shit." She walked away from me toward the bathroom. "He said, 'No one put lithium in our water. It's already there.' Just interrupted me talking to Darrin. I told him he was full of shit, right there in class." Water from the Coke can dripped onto the carpet.

She threw the can in the trash and turned back then smiled. "Darrin laughed at the profesor. He took my hand, and we walked out of the stupid class. We did it right on the staircase outside."

I rolled my eyes.

She pursed her lips until they turned purple, and she watched me for a while before she turned around to finish dressing. It was the same look she gave Manuela whenever she was begging on the street.

Manuela walked in drunk and dusty.

"Where the hell have you been?"

Manuela dropped herself on the couch.

I jumped up and hopped into the kitchen to get her some ice water and a cool trapo for her head. By the time I hopped back over to Manuela, most of the water had splashed out of the glass.

"¡Mira! ¡Mira! Esta conejita. You never get this excited when I come home!" Mom shook her head and went to finish dressing.

Alone with my tía, Manuela rolled her eyes at me. I nodded.

She lifted a hand and showed me her palm, asking me about Mom.

"Some guy from school—Darrin?"

She plucked her chin hairs with her thumb and forefinger, wincing when she pulled one out. I put the wet towel on her forehead, and she sighed.

"I've met people who have never had a job. All they do is go to school all the time; that's their job." I must have looked at her like I didn't believe her because she added, "Claro que sí."

"I'd rather work," Mom yelled from the bathroom. She leaned into the sink to get a closeup of her face in the mirror. "None of the boys in school have any money. This college crap has got to go."

"It's only been eight days."

"You mean I've already wasted a week of my life on this shit?"

I thought of Manuela and how she was out a hundred dollars on another one of Mom's whims. Mom had got it in her head that she wanted a college man. I went with her to borrow the ninety-nine dollars for the entrance exam from Manuela. It was the end of the month, and I knew Manuela had cashed her disability check downtown. We found her on Texas Street, with a man she had met in line at the Western Union office before she went into the bar. Manuela was more than willing to help. She told her new friend, "I'm not crazy for nothing," tapping her knuckles to her forehead.

Two short bleeps sounded, and I ran to the window.

"Get away from there, Gorda! Quit acting like no one ever comes to visit." Mom straightened the back of her skirt. "Ay, my suitcase!"

I ran into the bedroom and walked out dragging the baby–blue Samsonite with both hands. Excited, Mom kissed my cheek, took her suitcase with one hand, and walked out the door. I kept my hand on that cheek long after she was gone.

"You think schoolboy is the one?"

I shrugged my shoulders.

"Go get me some water, and this time no hopping." After she drank, Manuela sat. She held the greasy glass up. "You know, Gorda . . ." Manuela was the fat one. She had a large, round beer belly that made her look pregnant. "The drugs. The drugs, they work. I told the doctor, too." She always used the Spanish pronunciation for doctor, dok–TOR. "I told him I didn't have no money, and the pendejo just laughed. He said I should drink six hundred cups of water. You believe that?

"Este calor, it gets inside your head and makes you think different, slower," Manuela fanned herself.

"So that's your excuse," I said walking inside the bedroom looking for the Barbie that Mom took.

"Did you notice how heavy her suitcase was?"

I peeked out the door.

She saw me out of the corner of her eye. "I bet she packed all her shoes."

I ran to the closet to see if it was true. All six pairs of Mom's shoes were gone.

"You know what that means, ¿qué no?"

I buried my teeth into my arm to keep from crying.

"This is the one."

Manuela passed out on the couch and stayed there for two days, getting up only to sip vodka and go to the bathroom. I played kill-the-drunk with my Barbies, watched TV, and slept by the front door.

It was the middle of the week and still Mom didn't walk through the door. Anytime a car passed, I ran to the window and looked outside. I tried to remember the color of the car that I had spotted before she left. I couldn't. Inside the bedroom Mom and I shared, I looked through the dresser drawers. She had taken all her underwear. The only thing that remained was a triangular bottle of perfume that made all her things smell like lilacs. I put the bottle to my nose and inhaled—nothing. Then I made a deal with God. I told him I would stop drinking water, stop playing with my Barbies, and even stop wandering with my tía if he would just bring my mother back home.

Manuela screamed from the bathroom, "¡Papel!"

I ran into the kitchen, yanked a roll of paper towels off the spindle, and rolled it to Manuela through the open bathroom door. I sat on the couch thinking about how Manuela never left, unless she was having one of her spells. I thought about my mother, and how her life with us was never enough. How she spent her life searching. How all of us did. Manuela was searching for a score,

Mom was searching for a man, and I was searching for my mother's love. How the three of us would always be searching—searching for the one thing that would never satisfy us.

I hid the lotion from Manuela after her bath. The doctor told us Manuela's paranoia was triggered when things at home change, even a little bit.

"Where is it, Goddamnit!" Manuela's wet hair dripped onto the maroon towel she had wrapped around her thick body.

"Where's what?" I said, lying on the couch pretending to watch television.

"You know! You know!" She flailed her arms.

"I can't read your mind, tía." I kept my body on the pillow the yellow bottle was under.

"The crema! The crema!" Her dark face was so close I felt her breath.

"I don't know." I shook my head.

"¡Pendeja! You know." Manuela slapped my bare legs until I rolled off the couch to protect myself. The slaps stung.

The bottle rolled onto the floor from underneath the pillow. Manuela was shaking as she picked up the bottle, and for the first time in my life, I was afraid of her. I got up and started to run into our room. Before I got there, the yellow bottle hit my feet and tripped me up so that I fell on the floor in front of the door. She jumped on top of me and continued slapping me. Her towel fell to the floor. Mom walked in from outside, saw her naked sister slapping me, and laughed. Manuela looked up, I crawled away, and locked myself in our bedroom. My skin burned. Manuela cackled. Both women laughed themselves into quiet sobs. I noticed the bottle lying inside the bedroom, and I opened the door and pitched it outside, which started another round of hysterical laughter. I sat, head cradled in my arms, back against the door, and sighed.

Small Time

These potted palm trees, escalators, staircases, and tiled water fountains are as familiar to me as my own bedroom. It is inside this two-story sanctuary, in line at the lemonade and hot-dog stand, where mom passes on her secrets. I listen, arms crossed in front of me.

"Pick the men cashiers; they usually don't know what shoes and dresses cost," Mom explains with dramatic hand gestures that everyone in the Davilla family uses. "When the clerk isn't buying it . . ."

" . . . ask for the manager. Ya, I get it."

"What's wrong with you, Teresa?" She points at me with the plastic bag she is holding.

After a few moments of silence, I say, "I think I'm going to cut my hair."

"You've got a short neck, and short-necked women should never wear their hair up. It makes them look stubby," Mom says, slapping the underside of my chin with her fingers.

I slip the pencil out of the bun in my hair, and it unravels and falls to my shoulders.

"That looks better. Did you wash your hair? It looks oily, not shiny oily, but dirty oily," Mom says, while brushing strands of hair away from my face. "Ay, mija, with your hair down like that you have to wear more makeup."

"I'm wearing lipstick," I say, pointing to my lips. The gesture is so familiar that I stop and let my hand fall to my side and clap my thigh.

"Yes, I see your lipstick." She pinches my chin with her forefinger and thumb. "I guess you do listen. I can thank God for small favors." She lets go of me, and her hand falls to her side and hits her thigh. "I just have to repeat myself over and over. But, the color—pink? You're twenty-two, not nine. Your lips fade away with that color." She hands me the bag and digs a compact out of her black leather purse to reapply her lipstick. "What would happen if Revlon discontinued it?" she says, pointing the red color at me. "I'll stock up next time."

After buying a lemonade and corn dog, Mom sits on an iron bench to eat. I stand several paces away from her, opening and shutting the bag. A little girl, walking on tiptoes, drops an ice-cream cone nearby. An older woman leads her away by the hand, and the little girl looks back and cries. Seconds later, a man steps in the slush as he bites into a cinnamon roll. A woman in a suit, wearing tennis shoes, swings her arms high and huffs past us.

"You have to sacrifice comfort for beauty," my mother says, laying her food on the bench so she can slip off her new shoes. She places a Band-Aid on her raw heel. "Like I said, make a big escándalo, and they'll take it back just to get you out of the store."

I look down at my tennis shoes—the same kind the woman in the suit was wearing. Mom stands with a sigh, leaves her food on the bench, grabs the bag from my hands, and we take off for the store. Remembering the blisters on her feet, I slow my walking pace. We stroll past boutiques and fine department stores, listening to the Muzak version of "Mandy" over the loudspeakers.

Plastic, soap, and pine fumes attack my nose when we step onto the shining linoleum of the department store. The same crushed velvet couches that are in our living room are somewhere in this store, I think. My brother, Anthony, can do no wrong since the new living room set was delivered. This store brought the love-seat and matching couch right to the house. Anthony had used our cousin's credit card to buy the sofas. When cousin George had put two and two together after coming to our house and sitting on the new furniture, he and my brother got into a fistfight in the front yard. Gravel was scattered everywhere, and George got a raspberry on his cheek where Anthony used his foot to grind our cousin's face into the ground. Our next-door neighbor had to pull the two apart. He ran barefoot across the rocks that covered our lawn, while Mom and Dad watched. I had made fists with my hands and then opened them, "Come on! You can't be surprised that George is upset. Your son, Anthony, who doesn't have a job, can't just show up at our doorstep with the couches you've been dreaming about since before you were born." I had pointed at my mother. Mom and Dad were silent. They just picked Anthony up off the ground and helped him wipe gravel off of his arms. Since then, my cousin hasn't come to the house.

Mom's pumps clack, and she straightens her round frame and walks to the return desk. There are two people behind the counter, an elderly woman and a young girl. Mom takes a deep breath and heads straight for the young girl. The elderly saleswoman leaves. I hang back, hear steel scrape against chrome, women's voices, and my mother's high-pitched voice.

"Are you telling me I don't know where I bought this dress? Is that what you're telling me?" Mom leans over the counter and shakes the teal dress she has in both her hands. Lupe Davilla will not take no for answer. "You think I'm stupid?"

"No, ma'am, I never said that. I just wanted to be sure you bought the dress here because, it's just that, this dress looks worn." The tiny, dark-skinned clerk pulls on her nametag, with its big bold orange letters that spell "Esmeralda." The minute the words come out of her mouth, I can tell by the way she steps away from the counter that Esmeralda is sorry she said anything. She reminds me of Anthony when he was six years old, sitting up in bed, trying to keep his eyes open. Afraid. Afraid to sleep because he knew that when he woke up, all the money he had made pulling the weeds that grew between the bright gravel and cactus in people's yards would be gone. Taken in the dark by our mother. My head aches from hunger, the bright lights, and the inescapable smell of plastic.

"Oh, so now you're calling me a liar." Mom jerks the dress off the counter. "I want to talk to your manager."

I cringe. My mother looks radiant. Cheeks flushed. She gets a thrill knowing she'll soon have cash in hand. Mom can make money out of anything. She lifts books from the shelves of our neighborhood library. She enjoys making up stories about her dying mother, while gushing real tears, just to get her hands on quick cash.

Her credit cards are maxed. The banks, her brothers, mother, and father won't float her a loan anymore. She's nothing like her brother, Carlos.

"I'm a liar, you say?" Mom shakes the dress she holds in both hands and then slams it onto the orange counter top. "I shop in this store every week." She taps the counter with a red manicured nail. "And you can bet that after treatment like this, I won't be shopping here again." Mom points the finger she had tapped on the counter toward Esmeralda, "You know what, you can just take my credit card right now." She digs into her purse for her wallet.

"Ma'am, you don't have to do that," Esmeralda says, glancing behind Mom at the line that is forming.

Mom turns and winks at me. She has the same crooked smile as tío Carlos.

I roll my eyes thinking of tío Carlos, because he's someone I respect. He tried to rob the Credit Union. Would have walked away, free and clear, if his wife hadn't been upset. Tía Yoli had driven off and left him in the parking lot holding a sack load of money because she was still mad at him for cheating on her. He spent two years in prison, all because she was pissed. I remember how nervous Yoli was while waiting for him at the bus station in Huntsville. We all were. When he saw her, they ran to each other and hugged for the longest time, and just like that, all was forgiven. Carlos doesn't set his sights low.

"I've been shopping here since before you were born. This is the thanks I get for being a loyal customer?" She waves the white credit card in the air. Her close-cropped auburn hair bounces softly. "You know what, I'm sick of arguing with you." She points the card at Esmeralda, and my mother's coiffed hair moves in perfect sync with her actions. "Where's your manager? Let me talk to the manager."

Purple blotches form on Esmeralda's dark face. The English she has worked so hard to perfect becomes spotted with Spanish, "I cannot accept this dress, señora."

"Well, get me someone who can accept this dress, damn it! This is ridiculous, just ridiculous. I've been insulted and accused of lying. I'm not going to ask you again. Get me your manager."

I stand fast, in a fleeing, yet staying, position, feeling as nervous as I was waiting for tío Carlos's reaction to Yoli after he got out of jail. The week after he was out, he had driven up to our house in a shiny black Lincoln town car and had given it to Dad. "Those letters, ése. I looked forward to getting them every week," Carlos had said, then knocked fists with my father. I could tell Dad had wanted to hug him but held back. Dad washed that car every weekend. We'd all hop in and take a drive along the Border Highway, then park to watch illegals cross over. The car is history, just like this sales clerk is going to be. I look at the wrapping paper samples behind Esmeralda, then at the blotches on the girl's face. I match up the shade of purple to the square samples tacked to the wall, hoping no one I know would show up. Mom had worn that teal dress two nights ago to a quinceañera.

"Please let me see the dress. Perhaps I did not inspect it closely," Esmeralda says. She takes the nylon dress from the counter and asks my mother for the receipt, which of course she doesn't have.

Mom said before we got out of the car, "I don't need a receipt." Then she slipped the dry-cleaned dress out of its plastic, and we both ran inside the Mall because it had started to sprinkle.

Now, she empties her purse on the counter and inspects every stained, folded slip of paper she comes across, as the line behind her gets three people longer. She ignores the people, and unfolds the seventh and last square piece of paper on the counter, then says finally, "I don't have a receipt."

Esmeralda squints. Mom grinds her teeth then sighs. The air comes out through her nose, her shoulders lift then drop, and she never takes her eyes off the young clerk.

"How much did you pay for the dress?" The word "much" comes out sounding like "mush." People in line cough and sigh.

"It was one hundred and forty-eight dollars."

Esmeralda turns to look at the door behind her, then she looks again at Mom, whose argumentative eyes stare right back. She says, "Un momento, por favor," and walks through the door to find her manager.

I smile. Mom frowns. When the store manager arrives, he apologizes to my mother. She turns to me and smiles wide.

I frown. Thoughts of the Lincoln town car fill my head. After Dad had lost his job hauling chickens, my brother, Anthony, got his teeth kicked in in a fight. Desperate, Dad had called some friends to take the car from the Mall parking lot. They had driven it over to Juárez and parked it on the strip with the keys inside. "Leaving your chaqueta in the car was a nice touch, ése," Carlos had told my dad. "But Chuy, you should have wrecked the car. There's a lot more money in damage claims. Shit, you could even sue Ford, where the real money is." Carlos is always thinking about the big picture. All Dad had gotten out of the deal was a nice satin windbreaker from the insurance money—the rest went into my brother's mouth.

The store manager looks a lot like the insurance adjuster who checked on the Lincoln. The manager fingers Mom's dress then scans a ledger that's three inches thick. He finds what he's looking for, then punches keys on the cash register. The drawer opens, and he tears a receipt off the machine, scribbles on it, asks my mother to sign, then hands her one hundred and seventy-one dollars and sixty cents.

I say, "But—" then stop when I see my mother's jaw muscles relax. She looks just like she did when she tried on that pair of five-hundred-dollar sling-backs at Neiman Marcus then walked out with nobody following her.

Her eyes become the charming eyes of a hostess at a party as she says, "Thanks so much. I'm sorry I was so upset. It's just that I bought this dress for my daughter's wedding but that puto never showed. I'm still a little . . ."

"I understand, señor—," Esmeralda corrects herself, "Ma'am."

As we walk away from the counter, and as Mom puts the money in her wallet, I whisper, "I thought you said the dress cost one hundred and forty-eight dollars?"

"You're upset because I lied?" Mom holds her pocketbook to her chest. "Are you kidding me?"

I say nothing.

"Here we go. Esta Sandra Dee is trying to tell me how to live my life," Mom says to a teenager passing. The boy shrugs his shoulders. "Please, Teresa, enlighten me."

Before I can speak she says, "Well, you know what, they're big corporations, they couldn't care less. You know how much money these people are making off people like us? Do you?"

I shake my head remembering the seventy dollars Mom gave

me to buy the stroller for the quinceañera girl, who is four months pregnant. I stand taller because I still have thirty of those dollars in my hip pocket. The stroller had cost me one dollar and ninety cents. I smile thinking how easy it was to switch price tags. But still, my hands had been sweaty and sticking to the green handles on the shopping cart. I wonder if Mom ever gives a silent prayer like I did before I paid.

"They make more than we'll ever see in our lifetime," Mom says. "These pinche corporations even have money to cover shoplifting. They hire big fancy lawyers to get all their money back from the government. They don't pay no taxes—"

"You made a twenty-three dollar profit," I say.

Outside the rain makes the parking lot look freshly tarred, and the air smells like mud. Mom says, "Perfect."

Inside the car, I ask, "What's so perfect about rain?"

"The man is coming to see about our roof today."

"We're finally going to get the leaks fixed?"

"Better. We're going to get a check."

When we arrive, tío Carlos is under the eave of the house, where no rain can hit him, talking with Dad and Anthony. The cement driveway is dark gray. I smile and wave as Mom honks. All three men look at the car, and toss their heads back slightly.

Mom and I run to the door, and the men follow us inside the house.

"Get the ollas," Mom yells.

I walk into the kitchen to get the big pot Mom uses to cook menudo. I set the pot at the end of the hall to catch the water leaking from the ceiling. Mom, Dad, Carlos, and Anthony are huddled around one of the leaks in the dining room.

"You think he'll show?" Dad asks Carlos.

"Rain don't make them melt," says tío Carlos, then turns to me, "Hey, Teresa clean out my car, yeah?"

"But it's raining."

"¿Y qué?"

I sigh but do what he tells me. His car is spotless, but I find fifty cents under the seat. I walk back inside, and all four of them stop talking.

Mom points to the pot full of water.

"Why do I have to empty it?" I say.

Dad walks down the hall, picks up the pot, water spilling onto the carpet, and dumps it in the kitchen sink.

"What's up with him?" I ask.

"He's nervous," Mom answers, real snappy, so I don't ask any more questions.

Ignoring me, Anthony asks tío Carlos, "You think the insurance will go for it?"

"Of course. Everybody in El Paso is getting cheques," Carlos says.

"God provides," Mom says.

"When's he coming?" Dad whispers. He sets the pot on the coffee table and sits in a chair.

"Soon."

When the doorbell rings, everyone is still, and Mom walks to the door to let the insurance inspector inside. The inspector says good afternoon, and Mom offers him some coffee. He declines and wants to get right to work. Says he needs a ladder. Dad jumps out of his chair to get him one. When Mom shuts the door, she gives two thumbs up to Anthony and Carlos.

"He's mexicano; we're in!"

I hear him walking on the roof. When he comes inside, Mom points to the leak in the hallway. I am sure he is going to touch the ceiling and feel the wet paint, which Dad had applied only last night. Instead, the inspector asks, "Where's the attic?" Dad and Carlos take him into the garage. Mom goes into the kitchen and pours herself some coffee. She sits on the red couch and runs her fingers over the cushions. She stands when all three men walk back into the room. The inspector wants to know when the leak started.

Mom acts like she's going to sip some coffee but then says, "Chuy, you remember when the leak started?"

Dad smiles and shrugs his shoulders like he does before he's going to tell Mom why he came home late, "It was after that real bad hail storm. I remember having to get a pot so the water didn't ruin the carpet."

All four of us turn and look at the inspector. It's as if we're holding our breath. I hear drops of water sloshing on the carpet.

The inspector says, "Yeah, I've been seeing a lot of that lately. I guess these roofers figure it isn't going to rain here so why bother making them right."

Mom exhales, her jaw muscles relax, and she finally takes a drink from her coffee cup. When he leaves, everyone talks at once.

"I'm going to buy the coffee table that matches my new sofas."

"No, Lupe, we need to buy Toño a car."

"I am nineteen." Anthony says.

"Don't forget me, hermana. I'm the one who hooked you up," says tío Carlos.

"A bottle of El Presidente for you."

"That's what I'm talking about," tío Carlos says.

The carpet in the hallway is drenched, but before I pick up the pot from the coffee table, I say, "I want a Revlon curling iron."

Pecado

It was morning when I got the call from my grandmother, Honorina, telling me my great aunt, Isadora Marmolejo, was dead. I answered the phone in my living room and walked, cradling the receiver between my shoulder and chin, into the kitchen to get a look at the weather through the window. On tiptoes, and using both arms to pull myself up, I peeked over the sill above me, out the casement window. It was one of those days when it looks cold outside, but it's not. It was hot and windy, but the sky was a blanket of white. There was sand on the windowsill. The sand got into places I didn't want it.

"Sara, your tía . . . she's dead."

"What? How?"

"Un ataque."

"A heart attack? I thought she was healthy."

"Sure, she was, but también she was old."

You're old too, why couldn't it have been you, I thought, but I said, "When . . . when did it happen?"

"A las tres de la manaña."

"Who found her?"

"Tino y yo."

I cried softly into the phone and remembered my great aunt, Dora. My tía had a way of making everyone she came in contact with feel loved. Her small brown eyes and thin brows radiated happiness. She hugged everyone, embracing them with her large flapping arms and leading their heads smack into her cushioned chest, which always smelled of baby powder and sweat. And it wasn't just the typical hermana church greeting, either. Dora gave her affection sincerely. Not like my grandmother, who commanded

respect when she met people. Her head cocked high, Honorina
never let anyone hold onto her too long. She gave quick, tight em-
braces and never kissed anyone on the lips.

My grandmother said, "Ahem."

"Do you need me to pick you up, abuela?" I sniffled.

"No, I'll ride with Tino."

"You sure?"

"Yes, I want to get there on time."

"I could pick you up. It would be one less thing for Celestino to
have to worry about."

I thought of my great uncle at the funeral. He would look like
an undertaker in his suit. And it didn't help that he never smiled.
I understood why my great uncle Celestino had married my tía.
What I couldn't understand was why Dora had married Celestino.
His bald head was permanently bowed, awaiting a prayer circle to
lead. He talked for hours about saving souls, especially those of
lustful young girls, like mine. As if preaching every day at La Iglesia
de Otros Hermanos wasn't enough for him, he brought it home and
practiced on me. I often wondered if Jesucristo was the only topic
of conversation he knew. His marathon sermons about adultery,
greed, and coveting put me soundly to sleep. I had hated church
when I was thirteen, and now at twenty-five, I knew I would hate
the church service at Dora's funeral.

"He doesn't consider me an encimosa like you do."

"You're not a burden at all, abuela. I just meant—"

"Yes, I know what you just meant."

"So, what time is misa?"

"We're not Catholic! It's a servicio."

"Well, what time does it start?"

"Mañana a las cuatro."

"I'll be there."

Honorina let out a low, "Hrrmph."

"See you."

─────────────

The next day, while preparing to go to the funeral, I tore through
drawers and boxes searching for the crocheted velo—the one Dora

had made me for church when I was in elementary school. Dora and abuela had debated about whether the cameo-rose or spring-flowers pattern would be more suitable for my first veil. When they had asked my tío's opinion, he sided with Honorina, who wanted spring flowers. Abuela's back straightened whenever she told me this story, and Dora would laugh and say something, like, "Two against one, means I was probably wrong."

I came across my tía's picture inside the Bible she had given me, and I inhaled the scent of talc. She was in her kitchen when that photo was taken. I would eat two eggs with bola, some beans, and fresh tortillas in that kitchen every morning during the summers. After breakfast, I would sit and wait for my abuela, Honorina, to arrive. She usually brought a dozen fresh-baked biscuits. Celestino would eat six with honey still hot from her oven and save the rest for dinner. I had preferred Dora's homemade tortillas. After Celestino finished his sweet cakes, he would ask Honorina to take a walk with him to the corner store for a newspaper and a lollipop for me. Dora and I would stay in the kitchen making tortillas.

When my grandmother and great uncle returned from their walk, Celestino would sit and read the newspaper, while Dora, Honorina, and I loaded the truck with clothes, food, and ten dozen tortillas. Once he finished with the paper, he would change into his good suit and tie, and Dora would take off her apron and change from her cotton housedress into her one good dress, a brown polyester one-piece with small white polka dots. The dress had a white belt that cut her busty, square body into two symmetrical halves. She looked like Honorina, only happy.

Before we women would climb into the truck, Dora would place a towel on the seat so we wouldn't burn our legs on the vinyl. From the passenger side, Honorina would get in first, then me, and finally Dora. When Celestino got into the truck, he'd raise his arms with his elbows out and poke Honorina's side, "Elbow room. I need some elbow room, mujeres." All three of us would smile, and he'd start up the truck. The gearshift was on the steering wheel. When he shifted, he would apologize to Honorina because his knuckles caressed the arm she held out in front of her on the dash to steady herself. She would shrug "ni modo" and smooth her dress. If it didn't bother her, it didn't bother him, and soon he stopped apologizing every time his knuckles came in contact with her soft fleshy arm.

We drove for what seemed like hours, until the paved roads became gravel and finally hard-packed sand, then past the hard sand to the loose dirt, until we came upon the tin and wooden-pallet homes of Celestino's parishioners.

It was the parishioners I was thinking of four hours later, when I was still searching for the velo. I imagined their disapproving faces at the sight of my uncovered hair. It was the same look my uncle had given me the day he showed up at my apartment to take the clothes I'd cleaned out of my closet to give to his congregation. He didn't acknowledge my live-in boyfriend, who was standing next to me. When Celestino left, I found the velo, and I placed it on my head and laughed, folding my hands in mock prayer. Then in a fit, I'd said, "It's ridiculous that the women of the church, de La Iglesia de Otros Marranos, have to hide their hair and bow their heads in servitude." And I snatched the delicate white veil from my head and tossed it into the junk pile that was going to a second-hand store.

At the funeral home, I cursed myself for throwing away something made by Dora's own hands. As I stepped inside the hot adobe building, which had no air conditioner, the smell of sweat and eucalyptus nauseated me. When I was a teenager, I lived in fear of my tío. Whenever he caught me talking to a boy, Celestino would drag me to church, which was always filled with parishioners, no matter the time of day. He would make me lie on the floor near the wooden podium. Then he and his parishioners would join hands, encircle me, and pray. I saw up the women's skirts. The heat, my fear, and my guilt, coupled with the sweat and eucalyptus odors, always made me vomit. This was taken as a sign that my lustfulness was being cast out, and they would pray harder. After hours of prayer, exhausted, I would fall asleep and pretend to be asleep until I was safely at home nestled in Dora's lap.

Now, I steadied myself, then followed the voice of a preacher through the foyer and into the chapel. The small room was filled with Dora's family, and the people of the church. I remember their homes from my tío's ministry. I remember Dora's lectures, too. "Don't drink any water they give you," she had said, pointing at me. "Be polite and tell them, 'No, thank you. I'm not thirsty.' If you're thirsty, ask me for water. Don't eat anything they give you, but be polite. If you're hungry, just wait until we get home to eat. You remember what happened last time."

The first time I went to Moon City, I drank the horchata the family we ministered to had offered me. I threw up the rice juice, my breakfast, and lots of water. I had liquid oozing out of my mouth, nose, and backside. I even fell asleep while I vomited. Dora had never left my side. For two days Celestino and Honorina had been alone to minister to the parishioners.

"Ay, mijita, you gave us the susto of our lives," Dora had said when I was better.

She was the one the people had wanted to see. Dora lit up any room she walked into—even their houses with dirt-packed floors that smelled like shit, beans, and women who had just started. She greeted all the women with a hug and a kiss. Celestino followed her lead, saying hello with a reserved hug and a kiss, and then Honorina would embrace the hermanas. Celestino greeted the hermanos with the same quick stiff hugs that Honorina gave the sisters. He seemed older than Dora, even back then, despite the fact that they were both fifty-one. He seemed older than Honorina who was fifty-five.

My job on those trips was to occupy the children while Celestino prayed for the sick. After the hour was over, and I was red from standing in the sun, Dora would call for me from inside the one-room house. Honorina and Celestino walked arm in arm to another house, for yet another prayer, while Dora and I stayed behind. Dora explained to the women how important it was to boil all the water they used. She gave them the food and clothes we had brought in from the truck. The women thanked her again and again. Then they asked her to stay a while and drink a cafecito, at least until Celestino needed her. She always stayed. Those slight, dark women told her about their lives: How their children learned English so fast they left them behind. How their husbands worked hard and sometimes wouldn't come home for days. How they missed their families back home in Chihuahua, Monterrey, or Torreón. No one ever wanted Dora to leave. I always wondered what Celestino and abuela did during this time. The women begged Dora to stay, but she said she had work to do, and then finally, after their protests and a long abrazo, we would leave.

My head bare, I walked down the aisle, unescorted, feeling the weight of my uncle's eyes and the indignation of the five other preachers next to him. They sat at the front of the chapel behind the mauve-colored casket that held my great aunt and directly below the large wooden cross that was the only ornamentation inside the building. The seventh preacher, Brother Murillo, who was at the pulpit, tugged at the lapels of his tan leisure suit, and when he did this, the button below the collar of his shirt unclasped. I wanted to laugh but instead used my eyes to trace the cracks that ran from the plastic ceiling fans down the clay walls to the tile floor before I spotted Honorina and my brother in the middle of a left-hand-side pew. While eyeing the thick hair on Brother Murillo's chest as it tried to escape from the opening in his shirt, I almost sat on abuela's lap. Honorina would not move, so I squeezed past her toward my brother. Abraham slid away from abuela, and I sat between the two. As I did, my grandmother checked her watch. Not even in grief was she off guard, I thought. I checked my watch, also—six o'clock. The sweat stains on Brother Murillo's jacket told me he had been preaching since the funeral service began, at four.

Honorina's velo, with its pineapple pattern, matched her black dress. Dora had crocheted it. I had sat with her as she did it. She had wanted to surprise my grandmother for her birthday. Now, the velo was pinned loosely to the top of Honorina's head, allowing her chin-length curls to frame her face. My abuela had always been proud of her curly white hair. She boasted that the color and curl were natural, never mind the boxes of Clairol in her bathroom cabinets. I tucked my straight hair behind my ears. My tío, sitting front and center with the other preachers, was the headliner. He peered at me. I looked down, touched my bare head, and sighed. All the women sitting on the pews to the right had their hair tied in tight buns with their velos draped over them. They did not wear makeup. I sucked my lip to keep from smiling. I had cleansed my face twice with astringent to get out last night's makeup. The crescent moons of red nail polish I missed near my cuticles sparkled like nipple rings. Honorina did not wear any makeup. And my grandmother's sagging cheeks glowed without rouge. She looked radiant.

Honorina whispered, "Where have you been?"

"I was looking for my velo, abuela," I said pointing to my head.

"For two hours?"

I laughed nervously.

As if energized by our conversation, Brother Murillo lifted both hands in the air and motioned toward the left side of the chapel, where I, and the rest of Dora's sisters, brothers, nieces, and nephews were clustered.

In his rapid–fire Spanish he spat, "¡Pa' todos que no tengan fe en Jesucristo, traigo un mensaje!"

Abraham leaned over and whispered in my ear, "What'd he say?"

"For anyone who hasn't found Jesus, I've brought a message for you."

Brother Murillo delivered another of his fire–and–brimstone messages in record time—one hour flat.

Abraham whispered, "I don't *even* want to know what he said."

I laughed, and Honorina pinched my thigh with a liver–spotted hand. A pink welt formed on my leg. I imagined her bald.

Brother Murillo invited Brother Gregorio Aguilera up to the pulpit, and he promised to speak for five minutes. He wore denim pants with fluorescent yellow stitching and a white cowboy shirt with only one, round mother–of–pearl snap left. The rest of the snaps were skeletons of silver metal that caught rays of light and shot them out into the congregation.

"He says he's only talking for five minutes," I whispered into Abraham's ear.

"Thank God," he mouthed.

Brother Aguilera said he wanted to explain to the non–dead the three classes of death. His aggressive finger–pointing caused him to sweat immediately.

"First, there is the physical death, which we see right here," and he pointed over to the coffin.

I realized he didn't know Dora's name.

"The second death is the spiritual death—probably the worst death of all."

I checked my watch. It had been five minutes, and he was only on the second classification.

"The third death is the death of pecado," he pointed his finger in the air.

"Luckily, the woman in the coffin was not a drug addict or an adulteress. Otherwise she'd take the bus straight to hell, no stops," Brother Aguilera shouted.

Honorina sat straight, barely breathing.

After the third classification, the hermano asked everyone to stand and sing a hymn. It was a Spanish hymn I had never heard before, but Honorina knew it. After ten minutes of singing, even Abraham was mouthing the chorus to the hymn about redemption. Shouts of "Aleluya," "Jesucristo," and "Fe Aleluya" startled me, and the organ that accompanied the hymn reminded me of the Dracula movies I watched late at night on television. I thought of Celestino and stared at my great uncle, who sat up in front, facing the congregation. Honorina's anguished shouts made me wince. The men and women to our right raised their hands in the air. My grandmother did the same. I counted the seconds on my watch. I wanted to test my grandmother's faith. It was only two minutes worth.

"This is like a Bizarro World," Abraham, who looked more like seventeen than twenty, whispered into my ear.

I had forgotten that Abraham never came to the services, too young to sit still for so long. I felt envious of my brother, who looked lost. I watched the thick mono brow above his large eyes. It was furrowed in an attempt to recall the Spanish that he had left behind in the old neighborhood. A big organ solo ended the hymn, and everyone on the left side of the chapel fell onto the pews with a tired thud, while the right-side parishioners sat down quietly.

It was eight o'clock by the time the third preacher got up to recount, in one sentence, how Isadora met Celestino during the Depression. In another sentence, he talked about how she became an hermana at La Iglesia de Otros Hermanos in Moon City in 1950. He said Dora and Celestino had no children of their own but that the church members were their children. Then, in a twenty-minute sermon, he explained the life of Celestino. The congregation heard about how Celestino had ministered to the sick. Honorina wiped tears from her eyes, and I wanted to slap her. The preacher droned on about how Celestino's prayer circles brought entire communities together. How his healing hands comforted and healed those with TB, malaria, cholera, and who knows what else. I shook my head as this unknown preacher spoke.

"Why are there so many damn preachers? I don't remember this," I hissed into my brother's ear.

"It's a sign of respect to invite each preacher in attendance to speak," Honorina whispered in my other ear. "How easy we forget."

I turned my body away from her, and waited for the familiar pinch on my thigh. When I didn't get it, I looked over at Honorina. She was watching a blond man with a bulldog face who was walking up the aisle toward the brother. The hermano stopped preaching, and the blond whispered in his ear. The brother gestured to the preachers sitting up front, facing the congregation. They all looked at Celestino because he was the only one who knew English. The dark gray suit Celestino wore made him look thinner and frailer than usual. Honorina never took her eyes off of Dora's husband. After a few minutes of whispering with the blond man, Celestino announced that the service was going to wind down because another family needed the chapel at nine. The four preachers who hadn't had their turn frowned.

Celestino took the pulpit. It was the first time all night that he had smiled. It was a tight, horizontal line below his long hooked nose. With just fifteen minutes left, he invited the entire family of Isadora Marmolejo up front next to him for a prayer circle. My grandmother was the first to rise. She stood so quickly that I stood up with her. I tugged at Abraham's arm, but he resisted and remained seated. I sat down again next to my brother.

Up at the front of the chapel, twenty people formed a circle with Celestino in the center. They stood with their heads bowed. Some family members linked arms, others swayed side to side, and everyone had their eyes closed. They prayed out loud in Spanish, except for my grandmother who was praying in English. My grandmother's high-pitched voice rose above the rest of the congregation. Her English degenerated into Spanish then into talking in tongues. Those sitting in the pews bowed their heads in prayer.

"She's in a zone, man," Abraham said, slicing his hand in the air sideways.

I fidgeted, and Abraham bowed his head. Amid the high-pitched voices and prayer chants from the congregation, Celestino was giving one–on–one time to Dora's family members. Honorina never stopped shouting her prayers, but every few seconds, she opened her eyes slightly, and watched Celestino's every move on the sly. She had a look that made my stomach turn flips. That faded, hungry look lasted only a few seconds, but I knew. I knew she longed for my great uncle. Celestino wiped sweat from the folds of his face with a white handkerchief. Every time he lifted his bowed head to his handkerchief, he peeked at Honorina. The look in his eyes was identical to my grandmother's. I watched, mouth open. Then I peered at my uncle the way he had looked at me earlier. Speechless, I sat. Touched my hair. Picked up the Bible beside me on the pew. Opened it. Closed it. Then I tried to imagine my aunt Dora's life. I remembered every time Celestino and Honorina were alone, and then, I imagined what they did when they were alone. I thought of both my grandmother and my tío finding Dora at three in the morning.

Angry now, I stood. I marched, like a soldier on a mission, toward the prayer circle. The circle opened to let me in, but I ignored them, and I walked right up to my uncle, and swatted at his face. He caught my open hand.

"You liar! Cheat! Adulterer!" I screamed, but no one heard. The chants of the congregation were too loud. I lunged toward my grandmother, and a circle of arms caught me. I was wrestled to the ground, and Celestino placed his healing hands on my troubled mind, while the entire congregation, including my brother, held me down. The church was filled with a hushed but steady chant, while I retched and spat at my tío and my abuela. They prayed louder and louder until finally, exhausted, I lay there. The smell of sweat and eucalyptus made me gag, and I knew was going to vomit.

Inner View

$\mathbb{M}$oist under my arms from my sprint to the building, I walk through the double doors, and a blast of cool air hits my face. Rather than refreshed, I am nauseated. After I sign in with the security guard, I jog down the cavernous hallway, find the glass door I'm looking for, and step inside. I swallow and head toward the secretary, whose angular face and slender arms remind me of a TV news anchor. Her face, with its hard, porcelain-like veneer, shines under the fluorescent lighting. I squeeze the St. Christopher medallion in my hand, and her bored expression makes me more uncomfortable. I smile. The secretary's blue eyes give no warmth—all points and hard edges like a cube. She speaks before I do.

"You must be No-ella Boost-a-mont," she says, mispronouncing my name. "Mr. Richardson is expecting you. Please take a seat. He'll be with you in a minute," she says with her eyes already focusing on the computer screen in front of her.

I do as I'm told and sit on the leather sofa. The couch I rest on costs more than the car my father drives. I place my Naugahyde briefcase on my knees. The dark, rich textures of the room are gloomy and intimidating. I feel out of place, like I did in P.E. class in grade school, even a little ashamed of myself. I imagine the walls painted the banana yellow of our living room and think it would brighten up this dreary office, maybe give the secretary something to smile about. I remembered my mother's words as I got out of the car, "Pórtarte bien, Noelia, you're wearing a dress. Sit like a lady." I put the briefcase on the floor and cross my legs. The minute I do, the pointy secretary tells me Mr. Richardson can see me now. I stand as if to race.

The smell of coffee hits my nostrils before I see Mr. Richardson. My mouth waters, and I'm feeling comfortable despite the gloominess of the beige walls. Mr. Richardson is all roundness and folds. He reminds me of tía Ofelia's spoiled cat, Gertrudis. He walks around from behind an elaborately chiseled mahogany desk and shakes my hand. As he holds my hand in a stiff, tight clutch, he glances at me—from the diamante rhinestone barrettes in my hair, down to the discount–shoe-store loafers I'm wearing. Even though he doesn't say it, I feel it—cheap. He wants to get right down to business. Doesn't offer me a cup of espresso from the espresso machine behind his desk. He doesn't ask me about my trip. If I'm comfortable, hot, or tired. He wants me to tell him a little bit about myself. Why I would be good addition to Richardson, Richardson, and Stoddard?

Annoyed, I answer, "I've been the office manager of the credit union for five years. . . ." I can see Dad's car through Mr. Richardson's window. It's just behind the high–back chair Mr. Richardson is sitting in. Dad has parked across the street, illegally. ". . . and before that I was a checker at Big Eight, and I'm bilingual . . . " I stare out the window because I see my sister, Teresa, get out of the car.

She's probably had enough, I think. Everyone in the family is inside Dad's blue Chevy in this 100–degree heat, and Dad turned off the air conditioner when he parked. As I got out, he was telling Teresa, "Eres escandalosa. No hace tanto calor." Titi just lifted her thick black ponytail and fanned the nape of her neck, which was drenched in sweat. "You're lucky you even have a car to ride in. I had to walk . . . " I slammed the car door and ran across the street toward the plaza, grateful that I didn't have to hear the end of the story again.

"Ms. Bustamante? Is there something outside?" Mr. Richardson asks.

"No, no sir," I say. I try to focus my attention on his face, but I'm distracted by Titi, who is waving her arms wildly, and now my father is out of the car.

I had tried to convince Dad to let me take the bus to the interview.

He'd said, "I'll take you, no problem. When is it?"

"It's Monday," I said. "You'll probably want to rest on your day off."

"Rest? I can rest when I'm dead."

I cringed.

"Lunes, I'll take you to your job interview. We can all go."

"No, Dad really I can take the bus," I said, desperately.

"N'ombre, you shouldn't take the bus for such an important day. We'll take you."

I poured him a cup of coffee, and as I handed it to him, I said, "I already planned to take the bus. It's no big deal."

"What do you mean, no big deal." He slurped. "You crazy? How much will it pay?"

"I think $28,000."

Dad whistled, "With that kind of money we can get a new roof for the house. I'm driving you, so you can have some support." He sliced the air with an open hand.

I turned to my mother, who was folding laundry on the kitchen table, and shrugged as if to say, "Help!"

"It'll be all right," she said, folding my T-shirt into thirds the way I like. "You're going to want someone to talk to after the interview. This way will be better. We won't worry, and don't you worry."

I rolled my eyes in defeat.

Mr. Richardson swivels his chair, "Oh, I see—a family argument. Amusing, eh. I love the Mexican culture. That's why my wife and I moved here. Actually, my wife isn't too fond of this hot weather." He looks out the window. "They are such an emotional people."

"Yes, I know," I say.

I was pretty emotional when Dad announced we were going to pick up abuela on the way to the interview.

"We only have twenty-five minutes to get downtown," I pointed to my watch. "There's no time for this."

"It don't matter if you're a little late," Dad said. "It's just an interview, not like you're going to actually be working."

When we got to grandma's house, Dad made us all get out of the car to greet her. I sighed loudly.

Dad yelled, "There's always time for manners."

I didn't want to leave the air-conditioned car but stepped out into the heat, and as I walked toward abuela's gated yard, I noticed the padlock shackle was closed tight. I turned to look at Mom.

"So what's the problem?" Dad called out. "Jump it."

I pointed to my business suit and shoes.

"Oh, forgot. Titi jump it and go get Abuela and tell her we need the key so we can come inside."

"No, Titi," I yelled. "Just tell her to come out because we're running late." I didn't dare look behind me.

Abuela shuffled outside with the key to the padlock in one hand and Titi holding her arm.

"Titi, get abuela's bag, and shut and lock her door!" I yelled and got slapped on the back of the head.

"What are we late for?" Abuela asked, shaking as she tried to put the key in the lock.

One good tug would break the rusted chain that was cinched together by the padlock. I stopped myself from pulling and said, "Let Titi do it, abuela. I've got an important job interview."

Abuela said, "Titi, get my bolsa."

I loved my sister at that moment because she ran down grandma's brick pathway and was back a few seconds later carrying the large tote.

Dad said, "¡Mira ésta! She has one job interview, and she thinks she can boss us around now."

"No te preocupes, mijo, she's just nervous," Abuela said. I looked at my watch and saw that we had fifteen minutes to get downtown.

Once we got abuela settled in the front seat, Mom sat in back with Titi, Joe, and me. I sat in the middle on top of Joe's lap. It was coolest there. The air-conditioner was hitting me straight on, and my makeup stayed in place.

"Would you move your fat head so I can get some air?" Joe moaned.

"Shuttup. I can't go to a job interview all sweaty."

"Why not?" Dad said.

Titi rested her hand on my thigh, but I ignored her. "Because it's unprofessional."

"Unprofessional? If you're sweating that means your working hard. Any idiot can see that."

Titi rolled her eyes.

"I saw that," Dad said, giving her the evil eye through the rear-view mirror. "You keep doing that, and I'll slap you so hard you're eyes will roll back permanently. Malcriada."

"Dad," I said, and Titi started to place her hand on me, but stopped and sighed. "This is an office job. No one wants to walk in and see a sweaty woman inside an air-conditioned office. It doesn't look good for the company."

"At least they'll know you're working and not just sitting on your ass, drinking coffee."

"That's the trick, to make people think you sit on your ass—"

Dad said, "Watch your language."

"And drink coffee all day but in reality you're working, working very hard," I said.

"What's the point in that?" he said.

"It gives you more prestige."

"Prestige? ¿Qué es eso, prestige?" He waves one hand in the air. "Sounds like bullshit to me."

"Being late is not good either," I added.

Dad looked at his watch. "Ah, you're not going to be late, mija. We'll be there en punto!"

Grandma said, "I like my coffee with a lot of cream and sugar."

Titi and Joe laughed.

"The best coffee I ever had I drank with a gringa," Dad looked over at Mom, who smiled at him to go on. "My boss's wife. She had a shiny machine. Looked like it was made from rims. The good ones like at the car show Joe took us to. Remember mijo, the trokitas were my favorites and the bombs."

"I liked the girls the best," Joe said.

Titi punched his arm.

"It's true," Joe added. "And Dad didn't mind the view, either."

Mom hit his other arm, and everyone laughed.

"Ay, Dad, it's an espresso machine," Titi rolled her eyes.

"Yeah, yeah, one of those expression machines. The coffee was bien duro, but she gave it to me in one of those coffee cups you girls used to make me drink out of when you were little."

"Demitasse," Titi said, then whispered, "Idiot."

Mom reached over me and slapped my sister's thigh.

"Sorry," Titi said.

Oblivious, Dad said, "You were little, and you both wanted to make my coffee. You shouldn't be sorry. I loved playing with you girls. That's what the gabacha reminded me of, a little girl in a big house all by herself. She kept talking about this machine and how it was from France and what it did, when all I wanted was another cup of coffee, in a real cup."

We all laughed.

"Gabachos," abuela said, absently. "They love their things, and they're always in a hurry."

I tried not to look at my watch.

Mr. Richardson's watch was a gold Rolex. He tapped it every few seconds, while he spoke. "Tell me something . . . Are you of Mexican descent?"

"Descent?" He catches me off guard. "My grandmother's family is from Chihuahua, so, yes, yes, I am."

"I thought so," he says. "I'm sorry, please go on; you were saying you are bilingual."

My head is spinning. I wonder if what he asked was proper. If he just violated my rights. I look at this balding, pale man, really look at him. His eyes are the color of abuela's brass padlock. There's a spot of hair on his neck just above where his collar chokes him that he missed shaving. His shirt collar, starched stiff, is tinged gray with grime. He taps his Rolex, as if to remind himself he owns it. He seems sad. I wonder if Mr. Richardson's wife is alone right now—alone in her big house.

"Yes, I'm bilingual. I can type 100 words a minute and write in English and Spanish. Do translations."

I wonder why I tried to get here on time. I feel bad about my irritation at my father, who had grabbed my arm as I opened the car door.

"Remember mija, men don't like show-offs." He looked serious.

Mom added, "And don't bite your nails while you're talking to him."

My little brother Joe said, "Try not to fart like you do in your bedroom."

This got Titi laughing hysterically, and Dad slapped Joe on the top of his head, "Serio."

I was almost out of the car before my abuela said, "Wait mija. I forgot to give you this."

I glanced at my watch: 2 p.m., and I thought, "I'm going to be officially late for my interview," but still I waited. It took her a few seconds to unclasp the necklace that holds her St. Christopher medallion. I wanted to rip the thin chain off her neck, but I waited.

"This is for good luck," she said and winked. "¡Qué Dios te bendiga! He'll help you charm your new boss."

"Thank you, abuela." I took it, slammed the car door, and ran.

"You can translate?" Mr. Richardson asks.

"Yes."

"And you're Mexican American?"

"Yes."

"You don't look it."

"Thank you," I say, ashamed.

He smiles and clears his throat. "Most Mexicans I know have an accent."

"How many do you know?"

"Well, the cleaning lady here, and my gardener."

"They're probably recent immigrants or illegals. I've been here for two generations on my father's side and three on my mother's," I say.

"Fascinating," he says, dismissively.

A buzzer goes off, and his secretary says, "Mrs. Richardson, on line one."

He presses a red button on his phone and almost touches his lips to the speaker, "Tell her I'm busy."

"She says it's important."

"I'll call her back in ten minutes," he says, agitated.

I try not to roll my eyes or pass judgment, but I do. My interview warrants ten minutes of his time. I prepared all weekend for this meeting, dipped into savings and bought a new outfit, even shoes, and got my hair done. My mind races, and I imagine this man sitting alone with his wife in a large house. He probably doesn't even tell her that he's interviewing someone for a paralegal position. I'll bet they eat their roast–beef supper in silence, speaking only when they're in bed and turn off the lights. "Night, I love you," they lie to one another. It's what I assume Anglo couples do.

"Sorry about that. My wife calls at least three times a day. Probably wants me to pick up some milk on the way home."

"Bored?"

"Yes, I think, you're right," he says.

"Where were we?" he says, and the buzzer goes off again. "What?!" He presses his lips to speaker as he pushes the button.

"Mrs. Richardson."

"I'll take it," he hisses, then lifts one finger toward me as he picks up the phone. "Hello. Yes. How should I know? I only took two semesters of Spanish." He looks over at me and pauses, "Wait a minute. Hold on."

With the phone still to his ear he says, "Excuse me."

I picture a graying, slender woman on the other end of the line, wearing faded denim and turquoise jewelry. I can see her explaining to her friends that she wears rocks embedded in silver because she loves the culture. It's why she and her husband moved to the Southwest.

He snaps his fingers. "Can you tell me how to say, 'Please don't trim the rose bushes' in Spanish? My wife likes to trim them herself," he says sheepishly, "because the roses are Golden Wings from her Auntie Lem's yard." He covers the receiver of the phone with his hand and whispers. "She wanted to bring a little bit of home with her here."

I pause for a moment, smell the espresso, think about the secretary, the walls, the couch, how much translating I'd have to do for this man, my family sitting out in the car, and I say, "Sure. Here's what you can tell him: 'No riegue los rosales.'"

Love Web

Ⅰ stab my bobble-head Chihuahua with my pen and imagine I'm one hundred and fifty pounds thinner, my upper arms don't flap, and my butt cheeks are symmetrical, tight, half-moon slabs. My lover, James Morris, is always holding me by my sides, and I don't pull away.

Hungry, I get up from my desk, give my dog another poke, then head for the break room where there is always birthday cake. I think of James caressing my rock-hard ass, and I smile. He fondles my hair, which is cut in a soft bob that bounces gracefully about my face, and he admires my smooth, white skin. He tells me I remind him of a porcelain doll. I say something charming and witty, and I don't pick my nose when I'm nervous.

"Dora, right?" James Morris says, watching my fingers. "You answer phones?"

I nod, picking up a piece of birthday cake lying on the chrome and glass table in front of me. I can't believe he actually knows my name.

"You can have my piece. You need it to keep your shape." He pats the larger of my two cheeks, clicks his tongue, then gives me a wink before he squeezes past me. Actually, it is more than a wink. It's as if his hazel eyes had looked past the middle-age acne I can't find a cure for, the hole I had ripped in my shoe to relieve the pressure from my bunion, and the stain on my blouse from the breakfast taco I ate earlier, and they see the real me. Then, he hands me his slice of cake. Somehow he knows chocolate is my favorite. I take the piece off his hands and eat it.

He sensed the connection, too, because like a prairie dog in the spring, he pops his head up from his cubicle wall and waves every so often. I lose my train of thought, and I laugh when I see those elevator eyes. I decide I'm going to talk to him after work but this time I will have something to say. By five o'clock, I'm ready to leave but James is still on the phone. So, I pull out my EZ tax form and wait for him to leave his cubicle. A little before six thirty, he stops by my desk.

"Working late?" He scans my face, neck, and breasts.

"Yes," I lie, sliding my tax form into a manila folder.

"Dora, ah, do you mind doing me a favor?" he says, tapping his knuckles against his briefcase.

"What?" I look at him and stammer. "No, no, not at all. What is it?"

"Well, it's a little personal," he says. "I know you're pretty busy up here answering the phones and sorting mail."

"Yes, my hand gets cramped from all the messages I have to write." I hear his knee rap against my desk. "I also keep the appointment book for the conference room. Order supplies and . . ."

"Yeah, right. But would you mind screening my calls?"

"Why?"

"Well, here's the personal part." He leans over the four-foot reception desk. "There's this woman stalking me."

"Noooo . . . ," I say, like I don't believe him.

"It sounds crazy, right? I'm trying to hide from a woman. I didn't think anyone would believe me."

"No. No, I mean, I said 'no' like when people say 'get out of here.' I absolutely believe you. You're good looking, single, everyone likes you. I can see how a woman would want you so bad she'd resort to stalking." I turn red and cover my mouth.

"Exactly," he says, with a chuckle. "Her name is Lisa, and if you could just tell her I'm out of the office when she calls. . . ." He coughs and straightens up when another sales rep walks by. Before turning his attention back to me, he gives her the once-over. "If you could keep this between you and me, I'd appreciate it." He cocks his hand like a gun and points it at me. "Thanks, señorita."

He knows Spanish. I'm impressed. I want to say something profound but only manage, "Your secret is safe with me." I knock my forehead against my desk after he walks out the door.

"Twelve calls this morning from Lisa," I say, handing him his messages.

"Yeah." The telephone is cradled between his chin and shoulder. He looks up at me and opens and closes his mouth like he is chattering.

I laugh before I say, "You calling it off?"

He raises one hand and shows me four fingers. Then points his gun finger at me.

"I see." I jog to my desk to answer the phone. It's Lisa again. "He's in a meeting, would you like to leave a message?" I tell her, panting.

Lisa isn't a stalker. She is just a woman in love with someone out of her league. She makes herself available to James to use and abuse. And like most men, he takes advantage. She's one of the best sources I have for getting information concerning James. And I have to hand it to her—after two weeks of no contact, she is still trying to break back into the upper tiers of James's love web. It only took me a week to come up with the web system. It's actually a number system. I've numbered his girlfriends one through five. James only talks to his number one and two girlfriends. The other three have to leave messages. One and two are usually the newest girls, his favorites, and they don't bother him much at work. When they do call, their voices are still a low and seductive pitch, not yet the high, nasal whine of desperation that the number three through five girls have. The number one and two girls last, maybe, two or three days, and then they move down the ranks. I've gotten pretty good at guessing who's where on his list by the number of times they call or just by the tone of their voices. I always know all five by name, whoever they may be each week. He told me that he doesn't date more than five at a time, except for last summer when he dated the McGuire twins, and nearly got killed by the one that was a cop. When Suzy found out he had slept with her sister, she pulled out her magnum and shot out all four tires of his BMW. He says more than five is asking for trouble.

One of his girlfriends calls at least once a day. When the relationship is in trouble, it's more than once. I like talking to them. They think I'm his personal secretary, and I don't tell them any different. Aren't bosses always going after their secretaries? I have my favorites, too. Numbers four and five love to talk. They tell me all about James—how they love the dimple on his cheek when he smiles, how he has a thick scar between the cheeks of his butt, how his head jerks to the left . . . These women keep me informed. Let me in on the private life of the man I'm going to marry. And they like talking to me, too.

When Lisa calls back I tell her, "James didn't look so good today. Is everything okay?"

"Is he upset?" she asks.

"I don't know but he looks like he hasn't slept." I lie.

"Oh, gosh." Her voice sounds strained.

"What's wrong?"

"Well, I really made him mad last night," she says.

"Oh."

"James was upset because I wasn't home when he called."

Here it comes . . . .

"Gosh, I should have stayed home last night. If I'd had known. But he hadn't called in a week."

"Could you please hold? There's another call."

"Oh, I'm sorry for telling you all this. I really should be going."

"You don't have to apologize to me. I've been there. Please hold though." When I get back on the line, she doesn't stop talking.

"He reached me at about eleven last night, and he said he didn't want to have anything to do with a girl that was going all over town without him."

So stupid, I think. James is smart, putting the blame on her.

"He thinks I'm cheating. I'm not. I was at my mother's house, but he didn't believe me."

She's a goner.

———————————

Early Monday morning, Lisa calls the office and asks for me.

"I broke," she says.

"Oh," I say, disappointed, but not sure why.

"It hurt so bad," she cries.

And I know. James has his weakness.

Mr. Douglas's phone line is ringing. When he hired me, he told me that his personal phone line was priority number one, and if his secretary was out of the office, I should answer his line before the others. But I'm not going to let this moment pass me by. Lisa is going to tell me about the entire night, so I make an executive decision and ignore his line. I cradle the phone so tight my fingers ache. A slap on the counter distracts me, and I'm surprised to see James. He drums his fingers on my desk. He looks tired and smug. I cup the phone with my hand and whisper, "Lisa."

He points to his desk, which surprises me. She's made a comeback.

"Lisa, James just walked in, and he wants to talk to you."

"Oh, God."

She sounds embarrassed, but I patch her through. After that conversation, I know what has to be done.

———————

James brings me chocolates and a coffee mug the next morning. "How's my favorite secretary?" he says, sounding so nasty it makes me blush.

"Fine." I wonder if he was with Lisa last night.

"Any calls?"

The phone rings, and I answer it. I nod at him and say out loud, "Jane, please hold. I'll transfer you to his office."

James snaps his fingers and says, "You know this girl can wear the hell out of blue jeans. Her ass is a perfect heart shape."

Number ones, I think, are so lucky. That evening I go shopping for a pair of jeans. Come casual Friday, I wear the denim pants despite the problem with my ass. Everyone just stares. While I'm inside a bathroom stall, I overhear two of the women sales reps talking about me.

"Did you see her ass?" says the busty one James is always watching.

"You could show a movie on her right cheek, and roll the credits at the same time on her left."

Angry, I walk out of the stall and wash my hands. The busty one coughs, and the other one stops talking. Neither looks at me or says hello. They walk out of the bathroom together. These are the same two that got chippy with me when I told them I couldn't take their personal messages. "I don't have time to keep track of hundreds of personal phone calls," was what I had said. They had gotten upset, but I didn't see them complaining at staff meetings. What were they going to say? "Dora won't take my personal phone calls." They won't be getting any of their messages any time soon.

James didn't get to see me in my new jeans because he called in sick. He must have started an early weekend with Jane. After work, I drive home, take my jeans off, throw them in the trash, and feed my birds.

I've noticed that James misses a lot of work. He's partial to Mondays and Fridays. He'll miss one of those two days at least twice a month.

Monday morning, I bring donuts as usual—a special treat for everyone in the office, something to make the start of the week more bearable. Before I can take the donuts to the break room, I get called into Mr. Douglas's office. As I walk by, Busty whispers something to a co-worker standing next to her at the copy machine. When I leave his office, my head hurts, and I know my face is red, and I try not to make eye contact with Busty. She's still at the copy machine. I can hear its hum, and I catch bits of words. "Mrs. Douglas" and "upset." When I sit down, the barbacoa burrito I had eaten in the car on the way to the donut shop isn't sitting well. My stomach rumbles, so I get up, switch the answering machine on, pull out my bathroom break sign, and head out the double doors, down the carpeted hallway, and toward the women's restroom. I nearly fall over when I see the "do not enter" sign.

With no other option, I walk into the men's room. Luckily, no one is here. I run into a stall and empty the contents of my breakfast, midnight snack, after-dinner snack, and yesterday's dinner. As I'm finishing up, I hear voices. Embarrassed, I lift my feet, resting one on the toilet roll dispenser and the other on the door in front of me.

"Damn, smells like your house, James," Tony from accounting says.

"You jealous?" James says. "Yeah, it stinks."

I want to flush myself down the commode and disappear. I look between my legs into the toilet and sit and wait.

"Finish telling me about this Jane," Tony says. "So you got her home."

"She's unbelievable, man."

I hear the zipper teeth grind and a sound like the fountain at the San Jacinto Plaza. I try peeking through the space between the stall doors, but all I can see is James's back. So I give up and listen.

"We're going at it, when Lisa walks in."

"No fucking way!" Tony's urine sounds like rain hitting a tin can.

"Yeah. Actually, she doesn't walk in. She just stands in the doorway and watches Jane, who is on top of me, bare assed. I don't know how long she'd been standing there watching. All I know is we were already done, and Jane was slumped over on top of me, resting, when I looked toward the door. I smiled at Lisa, who looked like she was going to cry, and then she ran out of the house."

"Only you could get away with that."

"Get this. I thought Jane had no idea what had happened. Then she asked, 'Who was she?' You believe that?"

"You're the luckiest man on earth."

"Yup," James says. "Got rid of one and kept the other."

There is a moment of silence before I hear the metallic flit of their zippers. They both walk out, talking about something I can't make out. My mind is buzzing with new images. He didn't even wash his hands, I think. But God, what I would give to be Jane. I'm not his type. He likes those tall thin girls with no breasts. I let my legs drop and flush the toilet. I wipe my forehead with toilet paper because of the sweat that had beaded up.

———————

The most infuriating thing about Jane, besides the fact that they're still dating after four months, is that when she calls she doesn't like to chitchat. She's very business-like, asks for James and nothing else.

So, when she calls, I tell James, "Your wife's on line one." He doesn't get mad, just laughs and drops what he's doing to take the call.

I've been doing Internet searches on her. She's not a wanted criminal, and doesn't get parking or speeding tickets. She lives a few blocks away from my sister in a condo she owns. The secretary, Sheila, at the non-profit Jane works for thinks she's a saint. While we were having lunch, it took all I had not to blurt out something I would regret. But this support group I joined to meet Jane's secretary is not about bashing bosses but about helping us help ourselves. So I sit and listen to how Sheila's husband does not like to have sex with her. And how he suggested she take a lover. I mention how my boss has many lovers hoping Sheila will spill something, anything about Jane. Sheila doesn't know who my boss is, and I'm not supposed to know who hers is either. I do know that Jane likes her coffee black and she hides king-sized Snickers bars in her office drawer. She eats two, right before she's about to hit some bigwig up for money. And if she's out of chocolate, she raids Sheila's desk for any sugar. Apparently, she goes through the candy bars quick because after Sheila says hello to everyone at lunch, she says, "I'm going to have to stop buying butterscotch bites. She polished them off again. And didn't even replace them. Like they were hers. She's so inconsiderate." I nod, but the others in the support group admonish her and recite, "Let go and let God." I usually roll my eyes and eat. After an unsatisfying lunch, I get back to work and Jane calls.

"He's not in right now," I say, looking right at the back of James' head. He's standing up talking to Busty, one cubicle over. "May I take a message?"

There's a moment of silence before she says, "Oh, really. I was just talking . . . Oh, never mind, I'll call back."

I smile with the phone in my hand, and James looks over at me. He puts his phone to his ear and shrugs his shoulders. I shake my head. He looks surprised and disappointed. I try not to smile.

An hour later, James strolls by my desk. "Any calls?"

"No," I say, ripping open a letter. "Meet any one new?"

He laughs and shakes his head.

"You in love?" I concentrate on the paper I'm taking out of the envelope.

"Love." He pauses.

I look up at his face, and he's biting his lip in thought. All I want to do is kiss his open mouth and run my tongue over his straight teeth.

He scratches his head. "I don't know, maybe."

"She must be good," I say, then crumple the paper in my hands and throw it in the trash.

"Good? She's very good." He gives me the same puzzled look I get when I tell him in Spanish to keep his wolf eyes off my breasts and his paws on my body. "I'm working late tonight so let me know if anyone calls before you leave."

"You too? I'm here until midnight. I've got extra filing to do for Mr. Douglas," I say. "I'm going to order dinner. You want anything?"

"Really? Yeah, might as well. Doesn't look like I'll be going anywhere tonight."

"Not even if Jane calls?"

"Afraid not. She's at her mother's out East. She'll be gone for two weeks."

"Too bad." I smile.

———

I finished filing three hours ago, and it's already 11 p.m. If I don't make my move now it will be too late. And James looks tired. I walk over to him at his desk and place my hands on his shoulders.

"Ah," he sighs as I rub. "That feels so good."

"It'll feel better without this shirt." I stop massaging him when he unbuttons his shirt.

"Don't stop," he laughs. "I won't try anything."

"It's not you I'm worried about," I giggle.

He grins, reaches up and pats my arm to make me start.

Embarrassed I say, "When does Jane get back?" and put my hands on the back of his neck.

"Do we have talk right now?" he says and sighs.

I move my hands to his shoulders and rub. He sinks in his chair and sighs again. He doesn't want to talk about Jane. I may be the one to make him forget. He stands up to face me, but before he does he gives the empty office a once over. His eyes linger on the entrance before resting on my breasts. I don't mind that he doesn't look me in the face. He's probably sick of Jane's flat chest. I can feel his erection against my stomach, and he lifts my skirt and twists my arms to make me turn around. I know he's sick of Jane. I take his hands off my hose because he's leaving burn marks on my stomach trying to rip them off. I take off the hose myself, while he undoes his pants.

My panties barely at my knees, he shoves me against his computer terminal. I gulp air. I close my eyes to the pain and try not to make a sound. When I feel his body jerking to the left, I know it's almost over.

He falls onto my back in an exhausted heap. I'm horrified, hurting, and in love at the same time. I never imagined sex to be like this. And I never imagined I'd be this close to James. I lift my head from his computer, and I use my sleeve to wipe the oil spots I left when he pressed my face into the plastic. I pull up my panties, which are still at my knees. I don't bother with my hose that lay on the floor like snakeskin. When I look at James, he is fully dressed.

"Thanks," he says and winks at me. "I gotta get back to work."

He sits on his rolling chair, turns his back to me, and begins to type. I say softly, "I'd better be getting home." He waves without looking.

I grab my bag from my desk and head out the door. Safely inside my car I hug myself, lean my check on the steering wheel, and mouth the words, "No. No." After about ten minutes I start the engine and back out of the parking lot. I can see him working through the windows, and for a brief moment, I'm embarrassed. It passes, and I'm proud. I hope someone saw us. Too bad Jane isn't around. I can't believe that I made him forget Jane. I think he really enjoyed himself. At home, I slip into bed, his smell still strong on my dress, and I dream about our wedding.

I'm in the office early the next morning. James drags himself in at ten. When he sees me he winks. I smile.

"Has Jane called?" He flashes me the gun sign then adds, "Pow."

"No," I say, wanting to break that finger.

Vieja Chueca

Aurora and Guillermo Arrieta sat across from each other, elbows resting on a green Formica table. The only time they were together was when they ate. Aurora talked, and Guillermo listened.

"Estos mexicanos, they love their country so much, ¿why don't they stay there?" she said.

Guillermo ate his sopa in silence.

"Míralas, estas cucarachas," she pointed to a man who was sitting on the stoop across the narrow street, drinking a beer and combing his long hair with a large-toothed pink comb. "No hacen nada todo el día. Lazy."

Guillermo looked up from his bowl and gazed through the window at their neighbor, Verónica, who had stepped out onto the stoop. She took the comb from the man's hand and ran it through her wet hair. He grabbed her by the waist and pulled her over onto him, crushing the beer can between them. Verónica's robe opened and revealed silver-dollar-sized dark nipples. She laughed as she pulled at the collar to close the gap, and they kissed.

"She pays the rent on time," Guillermo said.

"That's the only reason I put up with her. ¡Sinvergüenza! Out there en la calle like dogs for everyone to see."

"¿Hay más?" Guillermo asked, pushing the empty bowl across the table.

After washing the dishes, Aurora stepped outside, with her broom in hand, to inspect her home and the group of children who had gathered near Verónica's apartment after she and her friend had gone inside. Every day, Aurora stabbed at her stoop with her wooden-handled broom like she was hitting stray cats. She hated the dust storms that blanketed her cement porch with a fine layer of sand. Nothing could get rid of the grit. Despite the throbbing pain in her arthritic knee, Aurora knelt down and scrubbed the slab by hand with the water she collected from her baths. Still, the dust found its way inside her home, settling in plates of food and seeming to seep through the pores in her skin.

It was the dust she had tasted when she was rushed to the hospital the only time she and Guillermo had fought. It was six days after their wedding. Aurora was still feeling like Guillermo's beautiful bride when his mother had made it across the río, and she had said she wanted to stay. Aurora had refused. Had said she didn't want that rascuache woman in her new home. Guillermo had his soft hands around Aurora's throat. The gun had been Aurora's father's. She had pointed it at Guillermo when he'd told her that her hate was as steady as La Migra that patrolled the streets at night. There had been a struggle and a shot. Aurora remembered that she'd felt a rush of water down her legs, and she had thought she'd wet herself. When Guillermo had seen the blood, he had called the ambulance. Inside the ER, he had held her hand. When the doctor arrived, she had whispered, "I don't want no blood." Guillermo had told her, "You have to have blood. The doctors need to give you blood. It's what they do, amor." Adamant, she'd said, "¡Óyeme! No quiero sangre. No la quiero." Guillermo had wanted to know why. Aurora had pointed to the dark-skinned nurse by the physician's side, "No quiero sangre de esos tramposos. Filthy cheats." Guillermo had sighed and had untangled his fingers from hers.

Aurora swept her porch, forcing the sand into cracks in the cement. All the children called her la vieja chueca. She had heard all the stories they made up about her. It was hard not to because her front door was only a few yards away from Verónica's door. There was no privacy in the projects. Aurora could hear the grunting noises Mr. Montoya upstairs made when he was using his bathroom.

This morning, one of the boys in the group said, "Ay, it was Mr. Arrieta that broke her leg. He probably hates her guts." Aurora saw him run a large hand through the ducktail of his red hair.

"No, man, it was brujería, pure and simple." Another boy

hopped on one leg then landed on the other. "It's the price la vieja had to pay a witch for getting rid of her baby."

"No, no, no." A chubby girl interrupted, her hands holding the lime-green Lucas bottle she ate from all day long. "Chueca fell off her steps, my brother saw it." She dusted the salt-and-chili-powder mix from her hands onto her shorts.

"It was . . ." the red-haired boy was distracted and laughed before he yelled across the street. "Can you do it or not?!"

The sweat from Aurora's hands made the broom slippery, and it fell to the ground. When she looked up to chastise the red-haired boy for screaming, she saw Verónica's 12-year-old son, Rudy. He stood in the yard next door, looking across the street toward his friends, who were gathered at his apartment stoop. His brown skin was as smooth as the glazed pots lined up along busy intersections.

Rudy ran past Aurora. He was careful to stay on the sidewalk that was farthest away from her dirt-packed lawn. She left her broom where it lay and walked unevenly to the edge of her property. "You get out of here," her voice quavered. "You get out of here or I will tell my husband that it was you that broke the gum machine in the lavandería. Do you hear me?" The skin of her white, flabby arm shook as she pointed a finger in the air. "¡Mocoso! ¡Desgraciado, just like your mother!" Aurora yelled, looking up at the Lord. "¡Ay, estos traviesos!" She pushed her arms out in front of her as if to show God exactly what she had to put up with.

All the children yelled, "Go, Rudy!"

The red-haired one held out his hand as he waited for Rudy to cross the street to slap it. "You did it, man. You're crazy!" he said.

Rudy slapped the hand and wiped his dark brow. "Nothing to it! You see! No bad shit has happened to me. She's no bruja."

"Just wait, Rudy." The skinny one did a dance spin before continuing. "The day's not over. Johnny didn't break his leg until the night."

"Johnny's a tonto. I held my breath when I ran past her, so nothing's going to happen."

The approach of the white mail truck dispersed the gang of children. Aurora heard, "Gotta go," and saw some of the children run toward the mailboxes.

The red-haired one asked, "You coming, Rudy?"

"Of course, he's not. He thinks he's all bad ass because he doesn't have a check coming," the fat girl said, spilling salt in the air.

"Shut up, tonta! At least I ain't no low-life welfare baby having to wait until the first of the month to have *my* birthday party. I have it on my birthday, the fifteenth, every year. See if I invite you."

Aurora laughed.

The fat girl looked over at Aurora before she threw her Lucas bottle at Rudy. It hit him in the temple. She ran away. Rudy rubbed his head and smiled at the red-haired boy, who was frowning. They said something to each other that Aurora couldn't make out, and the red-haired boy looked at Rudy a moment before heading to the mailboxes with the rest of the crowd.

Aurora shaded her eyes with her hand to get a better look at the boy sitting alone. He smiled at her, and she noticed that his hair was the same color as Guillermo's. It was also the same color as the dark, flat-faced indios who would run across her yard when she was a child. She remembered the endless stream of smooth-skinned Mexicans who took the clothes she hung out to dry on the barbed-wire line her father had tied between the house and a rotted telephone pole. She spit in the dirt, remembering her mother who cooked for the thieves. She shivered and rubbed the goose bumps on her arms at the memory of her mother's words, "You're a mexicana, too, mija. We just got lucky that my parents came over and not us." Aurora swore then that she would never make the same mistake her mother had made, letting the Mexicans take advantage of her. Now at seventy, she had kept good on her promise. She winced, and Rudy looked down. Her dentures, one size too big, poked through her thin lips. She groaned as she bent to pick up her broom.

A short while later, Verónica and her friend walked out the door.

"Thanks, Vero. Te veo next week," he said and messed up Rudy's hair.

"I'm counting on it," Verónica said, rubbing her finger and thumb together, which made the man laugh.

Aurora swatted the cement with her broom.

"You hungry?" she heard Verónica ask Rudy.

"Yeah," Rudy said, walking inside.

Aurora held her broom to her chest and shook her head. Guillermo's mother had been beautiful, too. She was from Torreón, like Verónica. The lines on Aurora's forehead grew deeper as she thought about Guillermo and when they first met. He was kicking a can across the street and wasn't looking where he was going. She was walking home from the panadería, with a large sack of bolillos in one hand and pan dulce in the other, and he kicked the can right into the back of her ankles. Guillermo said sorry, but Aurora pretended to ignore him. She saw his straight, blue-black hair, and it gave her goose bumps. Guillermo mopped the sweat from his temples with his fingers and shook them onto the dark asphalt. "¿Le ayudo?" She shook her head no. "Órale, trenzas, déjeme ayudarle. I won't run away with your bags." Embarrassed, she gave him the bags. He pulled on her trenzas before he took the bolillos.

The smile faded from her lips when she saw Rudy stomp out the door. He sat on the dirt lawn outside his home. Sweat trickled down his temples and onto the front of his T-shirt as he held his head in his lap. Aurora walked inside to give him privacy. She sat, then stood, looked around her apartment, and started to fill a green plastic bag with dirty clothes. She walked back outside, clutching the blue handles of the bag, and noticed Rudy in the same position as when she'd left him. As she walked the half block toward the lavandería, she felt his eyes on her. The small of her back was wet with sweat from the effort of walking. Aurora heard a loud whistle, and she cringed. Calling that boy just like a dog, she thought, and she turned to see Verónica hand Rudy a wad of money. Guillermo stood out on their porch mopping his brow. He had a face like a large, moist ball of masa with two raisins for eyes, and he was constantly mopping those small eyes with a handkerchief when he walked in the 100–degree heat. He would emerge from their air-conditioned room for one week every month, when he had to go door to door to collect rent checks and late fees. He didn't have to do much around the complex because Aurora kept an eye out. She was the one who told him when someone was going to leave without paying the rent, in which case Guillermo used his large, round, rock–hard belly as a wedge to get inside people's units when they tried to slam the door in his face. Aurora wondered if he thought of his mother when he looked at Verónica.

In the laundry room, Aurora was pouring detergent from a brown sack into the washer when she heard the bell on the door jingle. Rudy had opened the scratched white plastic door, and he stuck his face inside for a second before he was off. Aurora walked to the door and watched him. The sun, no longer directly overhead, made a short shadow of Rudy.

Aurora left the lavandería after she put her clothes in the washing machine. She knew it took twenty–six minutes for the wash to run through its cycles, and she wanted to get home to finish sweeping her stoop before the evening winds brought more dust. She saw a crowd of children peeking into Verónica's bedroom window. Aurora slowed down when Rudy spiked a sack he held and yelled, "Get the fuck out of here!" The children ran away, and the fat girl yelled, "At least my mom don't have to sleep with nobody to pay our rent."

Aurora stopped walking. Rudy kicked the wall by the window, then he ran away. In several slow steps, Aurora made it to Verónica's back door. Her knee throbbed as she stepped onto the stoop. She glanced back at her place. She noticed her porch was tinged beige with sand. Veronica's screen door creaked when Aurora opened it. A blast of cool air hit her face, and the scent of garbage made her hesitate, but she pushed past the odor and walked inside. The apartment was littered with dirty dishes, trash overflowing, and clothes scattered on the floor. The shelves on the walls were cluttered with crucifixes, candles, and figurines. She heard moaning and followed the sound into the bedroom.

When she opened the door, she saw her husband, with his pants at his ankles, on top of Verónica. His dimpled ass was the same color as her porch after she'd scrubbed it and it had dried, Aurora thought. The bed was a mattress on the floor. She looked down on it and watched her husband exerting himself. Aurora looked calm on the outside, but inside she was as confused as a roadrunner at night. She picked up a fork from a plate on the dresser, examined it as if she were going to eat with it, then walked toward the bed and drove the tines into the soft, ash-colored flesh of her husband's buttocks.

"¡Ay, Dios!" he screamed, pushing himself away from the force of the fork and deeper into Verónica. She held him in a tight embrace as he tried to scramble off of her.

Aurora looked out of Verónica's bedroom window and saw Rudy, whose eyes were as wide as Lotto balls. She laughed out loud, and he darted away.

Acknowledgments

It just comes out of her, you know, like a pedo.
—My mother's very accurate description of my writing style.

I have to thank my parents, Andy and Corine Granados, for passing on their fighting spirit and sense of humor. I would never have survived without them. Their patience and support have sustained me. And thank you to the other, better storytellers in my family: my sister, Becky, and my brothers, Joe and Abel. They happen to be afflicted with the same embellishment gene I have, which is so prevalent in the Granados family—they helped me to remember, forget, make up, and get through this book. Thanks to all my tías, tíos, first, second, third, fourth, etc. . . . . cousins who, when put together in a room, don't let me get a word in edgewise and who have kept me laughing throughout the years. My family was my first introduction to the art of storytelling.

This book would have never been written down on paper if not for the support of my husband, Esten Cooke, I'd still just be sitting on a barstool drinking rum and Coke and telling stories in a desperate attempt to make people laugh. And I married into a wonderful family of "yarn-weavers." I'd like to thank the Cookes, all of them superior storytellers, who have allowed me the opportunity to write and embellish whatever I feel like writing, within reason, in their weekly newspaper *The Rockdale Reporter*.

Another man I am thankful for came into my life during one of the most confusing times in my journalism career. I still say it was destiny, even though he doesn't "believe in all that shit." Dagoberto Gilb helped me to make the leap into fiction by taking an interest in my writing. In the middle of Gringolandía, I found a piece of home. Gilb looks like my father and acts like my mother, and he knows not only how to tell a story but how to craft one. And he passed his wisdom on to me in the most tender ways: by sticking his finger in his mouth and pretending to gag to let me know his opinion of a story, and with nagging reminders, such as, "When are you going to learn how to punctuate?" or "I can tell you looked this word up in a thesaurus."

I'd also like to thank the students and professors at Texas State University who were a great help to me when writing this manuscript. I am especially thankful for Tom Grimes, who not only takes everything in stride but helped me to maneuver my way through the confusing college bureaucracy that was so foreign to me. And thank you to Leslie Marmon Silko and all the other great writers who took the time to read my stories and comment on them. These are the people who influenced me and helped shape the stories written in these pages.

About the Author

Christine Granados was born and raised in El Paso, Texas. She is a stay-at-home mother of two sons and a freelance journalist. She graduated from the School of Communications, University of Texas, El Paso, and she has an MFA in creative writing from Texas State University, San Marcos.